"Ethan, why are you here? You never told me."

"I couldn't sleep, so I thought I'd go for a drive. I just wanted to make sure everything was okay up here."

"But the police are keeping an eye on things." Her lips parted ever so slightly, and the ache in Ethan's chest became an actual physical pain. "Tell me the real reason."

Of course there was more to it than that. More than he could admit even to himself. More than he could articulate.

Time was running out. He needed to put a stop to this. Now, while he still could. "It's late, and you can stop looking at me like that. I'm not one of your wolves, Piper."

She flinched. His words had hit their mark with the desired effect. "I don't… I mean…"

What was wrong with him? He was an idiot. Such an idiot that he kept talking when he should have shut his mouth. "I don't need a champion, Piper. And I don't need saving."

Teri Wilson grew up as an only child and could often be found with her head in a book, lost in a world of heroes, heroines and exotic places. As an adult, her love of books has led her to her dream career—writing. Teri's other passions include dance and travel. She lives in Texas, and loves to hear from readers. Teri can be contacted via her website, teriwilson.net.

Books by Teri Wilson

Love Inspired

Alaskan Hearts
Alaskan Hero
Sleigh Bell Sweethearts
Alaskan Homecoming
Alaskan Sanctuary

Alaskan Sanctuary

Teri Wilson

 ™ LOVE INSPIRED BOOKS

ISBN-13: 978-0-373-71932-7

Alaskan Sanctuary

Copyright © 2016 by Teri Wilson

www.Harlequin.com

Printed in U.S.A.

"The wolf and the lamb will feed together...
they will neither harm nor destroy
on all my holy mountain," says the Lord.
—*Isaiah* 65:25

This book is dedicated to the people and wolves
at the Colorado Wolf and Wildlife Center
in Divide, Colorado.

Acknowledgments

Many thanks to the best agent in the world,
Elizabeth Winick Rubinstein and her fabulous
staff at McIntosh & Otis, Rachel Burkot,
Melissa Endlich and the wonderful people
at Love Inspired, my critique partner,
Meg Benjamin, my writing bestie,
Beckie Ugolini, and my family and friends
for their unwavering support.

Thanks also to Sue Healey for naming
Shasta the wolf and Chris Meager
for naming the Pinnacle Hotel,
where our hero Ethan Hale grew up.

And as always, I thank God for the gift of
words, making my dreams come true and
allowing me to write for a living.

This book could not have been written without
the help from the staff of the Colorado Wolf
and Wildlife Center. If you love wolves,
please visit them at wolfeducation.org.
If I've made any mistakes in my depiction of
these beautiful animals, please forgive me.

Chapter One

"Who's afraid of the big, bad wolf?"

Piper's heartbeat hammered against her rib cage. There was just something about looking into the eyes of a wolf at close range, something thrilling that brought about an instinctual response. Breathtaking. Primal.

The animal stood less than a foot away, one hundred forty pounds of sinuous muscle, gleaming white teeth and ebony fur. A timber wolf, with penetrating eyes the color of Klondike gold.

He took a step closer.

Breathe. Just breathe.

The wolf blinked once, twice, three times. Then, without breaking eye contact, he rose up onto his powerful back legs, planted his front paws on her shoulders and licked the side of her face.

Who's afraid of the big, bad wolf? Tra la la la la.

"Big and bad, my foot." Piper gave the wolf a generous rub behind his ears. "You're a marshmallow, Koko."

Koko showered her with more wolf kisses, heedless of the fact that it took every ounce of Piper's strength not to shrink beneath the weight of his massive frame. At only a year old, Koko was still very much a pup and seemingly unaware of his size. And his power. Not to mention the intimidation factor that came with being a wolf.

Stature, strength and piercing gaze notwithstanding, he didn't frighten Piper. She couldn't remember a time when any of the wolves did. Years ago, perhaps. Before she'd ever had the idea to start the sanctuary. Before the first rescue.

Before.

"Piper! We've got a visitor." Caleb White, the one and only paid employee that she could afford, stood outside Koko's enclosure, eyeing their interaction with curiosity. Koko swiveled his massive head in the teenager's direction and dropped back down to all fours. "I think it's him."

Him.

Piper didn't need to ask whom Caleb meant. There was only one *him* whose arrival she'd been anticipating, only one *him* who mattered at the moment. "I'll be right there. Give Mr. Hale some hot cocoa while he waits, okay? With marshmallows."

"Sure thing, boss." Caleb's feet crunched through the snow as he followed the trail back in the direction of the tiny log cabin that doubled as the visitors' center and Piper's living quarters. For now, at least.

Once she got the sanctuary certified by the National Nature Conservatory and secured one of their coveted grants, all that would change. She'd have the funding she needed to make this place everything she dreamed it could be. And the first step in making that happen was to get the support of her new home, Aurora, Alaska.

That's where Ethan Hale, a journalist for the *Yukon Reporter* newspaper, came in. Or so she hoped.

She fastened the double gates of Koko's enclosure and gave the wolf a final wave. "Wish me luck."

Koko loped to the fence and poked his slender muzzle

through the chain link. Piper felt the wolf's gaze on her back for the duration of her walk to the visitors' center. Of all the animals she'd rescued—from the turtles she'd gathered from the middle of the Colorado streets and carried to safety at the side of the road when she was a little girl, to the wolves she'd driven hundreds of miles to pick up and bring back to the sanctuary—Koko was her favorite. He was special. He'd needed rescue, perhaps more than the rest. He remembered where he'd come from.

Wolves never forgot. Neither did she.

When she reached the log cabin, she brushed the snow and straw from Koko's paws off the shoulders of her parka and sent up one last silent prayer. *Please, God. We need this.* Then she pushed open the door, prepared to greet Ethan Hale with her warmest, most welcoming smile.

He stood inside the cozy cabin, clad in a brandy-colored parka with a fur-trimmed hood, frowning into his cocoa. Piper felt like frowning herself at the sight of that fur. It looked an awful lot like coyote. Or possibly even wolf, which was too revolting to even consider.

But this was Alaska, not a fashion runway. Things were different this close to the Arctic Circle. She knew that. Still…

She averted her eyes from the parka's hood. "Good morning. You must be Mr. Hale."

He looked up and pinned her with an impassive stare from the most luminous set of eyes she'd ever seen. They were a mysterious, fathomless gray, set off by lashes as black as raven wings. It was rather like looking into the eyes of a wolf. Not just any wolf, but an alpha.

Cool. Confident. Intense.

She blinked, and felt fluttery all of a sudden, as if she'd swallowed a jarful of the Arctic white butterflies that sometimes drifted on Alaska's purple twilight breeze.

That was odd. Odd and more than a little bit unsettling. She'd never reacted to a man on first sight in such a way before. Certainly not in the months since Stephen.

Her heart gave a little clench. Now was not the time to examine such things. And this man in particular should not be giving her butterflies. First off, there was the matter of the suspect fur-trimmed hood. Secondly, he was here to be wooed by the wolves. Not her.

"You're Ms. Quinn, I take it?" he asked flatly. Clearly he was in no mood to be wooed. By anyone.

"Call me Piper. Please." She smiled and waited for him to reciprocate. He didn't. "So, um, thank you so much for coming. I'm thrilled that the paper has agreed to run a story on the work we do here at the Aurora Wolf and Wildlife Sanctuary."

He said nothing, just kept appraising her with those enigmatic eyes of his. The mug in his hand was piled high with an almost comical tower of marshmallows. They'd begun to melt, drip over the rim and onto Ethan Hale's massive hand. Good old Caleb. The boy was such a sweetheart. He even picked flowers from the grounds on occasion and brought them to her. The vase of violet bell-shaped blossoms resting in the center of her kitchen table was just such a bouquet.

She reached for a napkin, handed it to the reporter and tried to imagine him picking flowers for someone. Not likely. "Sorry. I think my helper may have gone a little overboard with the marshmallows."

"Thanks." He traded her the mug for the napkin and dabbed at the sticky mess. "Your *helper*? Singular? You have no other employees?"

"No, just the one." Why did she feel the need to apologize? Again. This time, for her lack of help. "For now. Although the youth program at Aurora Community Church has been a real help since I've moved in. They spent an entire Saturday here last week putting up the fences."

"High school students? You plan on staffing this place with minors?" He reached into his pocket, pulled out a notepad and wrote something down.

Piper couldn't bring herself to look and see what that something was. "A larger staff is one of the improvements I plan to make once we've been accredited by the National Nature Conservatory."

He lifted a dubious brow. "Your facility has been open for only five days, and you already meet the standards for an NNC grant?"

She'd expected to have to explain what exactly the NNC was and the types of monetary aid they provided for ecological programs that qualified, but it appeared Mr. Hale had already done his homework.

Good, she told herself. *Maybe this means he understands how important this is. He gets it.*

"Not yet." She cleared her throat. "These things take time. I'm still putting together the necessary paperwork. But applying for certification is my immediate goal, because once we have NNC approval, we can provide care for animals on the endangered list."

He crossed his arms. She'd just confessed her dearest wish, and he didn't look the least bit impressed. "So you intend to bring more species into the area."

"I hope so."

He glanced out a frost-covered window toward the enclosures. "Will these additional animals be dangerous predators, as well?"

Dangerous predators?

Maybe he didn't get it, after all.

"While wolves are indeed predators, I wouldn't be so quick to call them dangerous. Particularly rescued wolves living in captivity." Her hands were shaking. She forced a smile. "Unless you're a bunny rabbit."

"Or a child." A muscle in his jaw twitched, and suddenly it seemed as though the most dangerous predator in Alaska was Ethan Hale himself.

How was this interview going so horribly wrong when he'd yet to set eyes on a single one of the animals?

Yes! That was the answer. He simply needed to see the wolves for himself, then he would realize they weren't the ravenous, bloodthirsty monsters that he was apparently imagining.

"Why don't I give you a tour of the sanctuary? I think that will put to rest any worries you might have." At least she hoped it would. At the rate things were going, she wasn't quite sure.

He walked wordlessly out the door and into the snow. Piper took a deep breath and followed. The crisp morning air swirled with snowflakes as she led him down the path toward the wolf enclosures, their footsteps muffled by a blanket of pine needles. When she paused at the first metal gate and turned to look at Ethan Hale, snow had already begun to frost the tips of his dark eyelashes. He looked less angry out here, beneath the snow-covered blue boughs of the hemlock trees. As if he belonged here, in Alaska's white, wild outdoors.

She wished he were less handsome. Disliking him would have been easier, and so far, he hadn't given her much reason to like him.

She looked away and focused instead on the white wolf peering at them from behind the chipped gray bark of an aspen tree. "This is Tundra. She's an Arctic wolf, and it looks as though she's decided to play hard to get."

He squinted into the wind. "I don't see anything."

"She's behind the tree. Look for the pair of copper eyes blinking back at you."

"There she is. Her white coat is quite striking in the snow." A hint of a smile creased his rugged face and then vanished as quickly as it had appeared.

Those annoying butterflies began to dance again. Piper assured herself they'd reappeared only because she'd succeeded in drawing a smile from him, if just for a fleeting moment.

"She's a beauty." Piper reached into her pocket for a chunk of dried meat. "Here, toss this over the fence."

He eyed her open palm for a second before reaching for the treat with fingertips that felt unexpectedly warm in the frosty air.

"Go ahead. Give it a good throw."

He did, and Tundra charged out from behind the aspen tree in a flurry of kicked-up snow and powder-white fur. She leaped a foot off the ground, a flying snow angel, and caught the treat midair.

"Impressive," he said.

"Would you believe that until three months ago, she'd never been outdoors? A pair of college kids in Canada got her as a pup from an illegal breeder and decided to keep her as a pet—" Piper paused "—in the bathtub of their dorm."

Ethan Hale's brows rose. "The bathtub?"

"The bathtub. They fed her mainly pizza and leftovers from the dorm cafeteria. They thought it was cute. Then she grew into an adolescent wolf." Piper watched Tundra make a sweeping circle around the perimeter of her enclosure. Piper could have stood in the same spot all day, watching this wolf run. Free at last. "Tundra has no idea how to live in nature like a real wolf. She'd never survive on her own. But wolves are wild animals and aren't meant to be pets, either. Wild is wild. This place is her last resort."

"How'd she get here?" he asked.

"I drove to Edmonton and picked her up."

The corner of Ethan's lips quirked up. It was only a half smile this time, but she'd take what she could get. "You drove to the middle of Canada to rescue a wolf from a dorm bathroom?"

Piper shrugged. "How else was she going to get here?"

He looked at her with an expression she couldn't quite decipher. "I suppose you have a point."

"Come on, I'll show you the others."

As they walked from one enclosure to the next, she gave him a brief history of each wolf—its age, type, where it had come from and the circumstances that had led to its rescue. She explained that so far, the sanctuary was home to two wolf species—the Arctic and the Timber. Once the rescue center was accredited, she planned to provide sanctuary for the Mexican Gray wolf, as it was in serious danger of extinction. There were only seventy-five of them left in the wild.

If this sad fact tugged on Ethan Hale's heartstrings in any way, he gave no indication. Piper was beginning to wonder if he even had a heart.

But she'd saved the best for last—Koko. He pranced right up to the fence to greet them, ears pricked forward, ebony coat dusted with snow. Beside her, the reporter tensed as Koko pushed his muzzle through the chain link.

"Are they always so...so..." Ethan frowned. Piper wouldn't have thought it possible for a face so handsome to frown any harder. Yet somehow the tense set of his stony jaw made him appear even more mysterious. Impassioned. Alpha-esque.

Good grief. What was wrong with her? She'd been hanging around wolves too long. Clearly.

"I suppose the word I'm looking for is *agitated*." Something flickered in the restless depths of his moody gray eyes. "They seem borderline aggressive. Are the wolves always this wound up?"

Are you?

"Actually, a more appropriate description would be playful. Not agitated." Piper smiled as sweetly as she could manage, given the circumstances—the circumstances being that the future of her wolf sanctuary, her lifelong dream, now rested on whatever this…this arrogant jerk decided to write in his newspaper.

How had it come to this? She'd packed up and moved from Colorado to Alaska with little more than the clothes on her back and a trailerful of rescued wolves. She'd spent every penny she had on this place. She'd taken a leap of faith. Didn't God normally like that sort of thing?

She hadn't been running away, no matter how badly things had ended with Stephen. She'd been running toward something. Her future. And now a very large part of that future depended on this interview, this interview that was going so horribly wrong.

She lifted her chin and did her best to ignore the way Ethan Hale was looking at her as if she'd lost her mind. "And the answer to your question is no. They're not always this active. It's the weather. Wolves love a pretty snowfall. Doesn't everyone?"

Ethan scribbled something in his notebook, again without cracking a smile.

Not everyone. Obviously.

Piper couldn't let the tour end this way. She just couldn't. This man needed to meet a wolf, one on one. He needed to look into Koko's eyes and see him the way that she did.

"Let's go." She unfastened the lock on the first gate, held the door open and waited for Ethan to follow.

"What?" He stood rooted to the spot. "Where is it that you think you're going?"

"Inside, of course." She motioned toward Koko, watching the two of them with keen interest. "And you're coming with me."

Ethan stared at Piper. Standing in the snow with her blond hair whipping in the wind, framed by evergreens and wolves moving among the shadows, she looked like Red Riding Hood come to life. Then again, maybe her crimson parka was messing with his head.

"Come on." She beckoned to him, as if he'd been waiting his whole life to follow her into a wolf den.

"Right." He rolled his eyes. She couldn't possibly be serious.

By all appearances, she was. She stood staring at him, holding the first of two metal barred gates open. Waiting.

"I don't think so," he said grimly, and turned to leave, to go back to his cubicle in the newsroom where he couldn't feel the kiss of snow on his face or smell the perfume of alder wood and forest that had once clung to his skin, his hair and every piece of clothing he'd ever worn. Back to a place where he wouldn't be forced to remember things best left forgotten.

"Suit yourself," she called out from behind him.

He heard the gate clang closed. Good, she'd come to her senses and was back on this side of the fence, where any reasonable person belonged.

He kept walking. He'd already been here too long. Where had the day gone? He'd unwittingly spent more than three hours listening to Piper wax poetic about her wolves. How on earth had he let that happen?

Without turning around, he held up his hand in a parting wave. "Goodbye, Ms. Quinn."

"I asked you to call me Piper, remember?" She sounded farther away than she should have.

Then Ethan heard the jingle of keys.

Gut clenching, he turned around. Sure enough, she was unlocking the second gate, about to step right inside the enclosure. With the wolf. "What do you think you're doing?"

"I told you." She shrugged. "I'm going inside."

"No, you're not." Ethan had no intention of watching her walk in there by herself. Alone. Behind two locked gates where he couldn't get to her if something went wrong.

Leave it. She's a grown woman.

Clearly she'd done this before, and she'd lived to tell about it. But wolves weren't pets. They weren't dogs, cats or harmless little hamsters. They were wild animals. *Wild is wild.* She'd said so herself.

"I know what I'm doing, Mr. Hale. There's nothing to be afraid of." An unspoken challenge glimmered in her eyes. Eyes the color of glaciers in springtime.

Afraid? What did she think he was afraid of? Death?

Death would have been easy. Survival, on the other hand, had been far more difficult. Even now, five years later, he still wished it had been him. It *should* have been him.

He crossed his arms. "Do I look scared?"

The only thing he was afraid of was watching her put her life on the line. He'd seen this sort of thing go badly before. Once. And once had been more than enough.

"Actually, no. You look angry." She turned the key. Even from where he stood, Ethan could hear the padlock release. "You know, the company of an animal is scientifically proven to lower blood pressure."

"I highly doubt that applies to wild animals. Kittens, yes. Wolves, not so much." Nor pretty blonde animal rescuers. In fact, right now, it was a toss-up as to which one of them was a bigger pain in his neck—the wolf or Piper.

"You'll never know unless you give it a try." She glanced at the dark wolf standing just on the other side of the unlocked gate.

Ethan stared at Koko.

The wolf looked back at him with the same cool detachment Ethan had seen in the eyes of other wild animals. Wolves. Mountain lions. Bears. One bear in particular.

Bile rose to the back of Ethan's throat.

"I'm going in. It's now or never." Piper raised an expectant brow.

As much as Ethan wanted to leave, to climb in his car and head back down the mountain, he couldn't. Not if it meant leaving her locked in a pen with a wolf.

"Fine." He stomped back toward the enclosure.

Piper beamed at him, entirely too pleased with herself. Ethan just shook his head and tried to slow the adrenaline pumping through his system. Every nerve in his body was on high alert, prepared to deal with the worst.

She locked the first gate behind him, and suddenly it was just the two of them in the small fenced-in space between the double entrances. She stood close enough for him to see tiny flecks of green in her blue eyes. Nature looking back at him. Her hair whipped in the wind, a halo of spun gold.

Ethan nearly forgot about the wolf standing behind her.

"There are a few rules before we go inside." Her voice went soft, as if she felt it, too—the unexpected intimacy of the moment.

The wolf moved behind her, a shifting shadow in the violet Alaskan light, catching Ethan's eye. "I'd imagine there are."

"When we walk inside, just ignore him. Let Koko come to you on his own terms."

In other words, don't go chasing the wolf. "Got it."

"He may get up on his hind legs and put his front paws on your shoulder. This means he's curious, not aggressive. Whatever you do, don't push him away."

Ethan didn't have a problem with this particular rule, either. If the wolf wanted to slow dance with him, so be it. At least it meant he would be the only one in harm's way. Not her.

"And he will definitely lick your mouth."

Ethan rolled his eyes. "Oh, joy."

"It's how wolves greet each other. Just keep your mouth closed, and you'll be fine. Don't turn your face away under any circumstances."

Now the rules were getting a little strange. "You're telling me to stand there and let a one-hundred-and-twenty-pound wolf kiss me on the mouth?"

"One hundred and forty," she corrected.

"Even better."

She ignored his sarcasm. "And yes, let him lick your face. It's customary wolf behavior. Koko's an alpha. If you turn away, he'll be highly offended."

And would that really be such a tragedy? "Got it."

"Good." She shot him a dazzling smile. "Then we're ready."

She turned around to slide the padlock off the interior gate. Without even realizing what he was doing, Ethan reached for her elbow. His touch said what his lips wouldn't.

Don't.

Stay here. With me.

But she didn't notice. The moment his fingertips brushed the rich red fabric of her parka, she moved out of his reach. The look on Piper's face—the rosy cheeks, the slight parting of her lips, the breathless anticipation—it wasn't about him. It was about the wild animal waiting on the other side of the fence.

He'd mistaken the moment for something it wasn't. Which was fine, really. He had nothing to offer anyone. Not anymore. Not even the first woman to capture his attention in as long as he could remember.

Anyway, attention and attraction weren't one and the same. Sure, he found Piper Quinn interesting. Who wouldn't? He also found her headstrong and impetuous. He knew her type. She was a crusader.

So was he, and the two of them happened to be on opposite sides of the crusade.

Fine. This whole ordeal would be over within a matter of minutes. Once he'd seen her walk safely back to her little log cabin, he could drive away, write his article and forget he'd ever set foot in her wolf sanctuary.

"Hey there, Koko." She spoke in matter-of-fact tones to the wolf, as if the two of them were old friends.

Koko gave her a cursory glance and then trotted straight for Ethan. He barely made his way inside the enclosure before the wolf rose up on his back legs, just as Piper had predicted, and planted his massive front paws on Ethan's shoulders. It had been less than five minutes since she'd talked him into this escapade, and already there was a wolf breathing down his neck. Literally.

Ethan didn't feel panicked. Nor particularly threatened. The creature was simply curious, just as Piper had said he would be. Ethan knew as much. But that didn't mean he enjoyed it.

"Magnificent, isn't he?" she asked.

Once Koko had dropped back down to all fours, Ethan responded, "He's something, all right."

"Come sit down." She strode toward a fallen log near the center of the enclosure.

He followed, took a seat beside her on the log and braced himself for another lick on the face. But Koko seemed more interested in Ethan's feet. The wolf systematically sniffed his right shoe from toe to heel, then moved to the left. Once he'd thoroughly inspected that one, he returned to Ethan's right shoe and began the behavior all over again.

Piper laughed. "Wow, he really likes your shoes. Do you have pets at home? A dog maybe?"

"No." Ethan shook his head. "No pets."

The wolf began to tug on one of his shoelaces. He took a bite, and the lace snapped in two. Ethan didn't particularly care. Although he was slightly worried about losing the entire shoe, his foot included.

"I'm sorry." She frowned. "I haven't seen him do that before. He's not hurting you, is he?"

"No." Ethan shook his head. Koko pressed his nose so hard against his ankle that he could feel the heat of the wolf's breath beneath both his wool sock and the leather of his hiking boot.

Ethan grew very still. His thoughts were beginning to spin in a direction he didn't like.

No. Impossible. It can't be.

Then he looked into Koko's eyes, and knew that however much he tried to pretend that the wolf's interest in his shoes was arbitrary, that wasn't the case. His odd behavior was no coincidence.

The wolf *knew.*

A chill ran up and down Ethan's spine. He pulled his foot away, but Koko's jaws had already clamped down. Hard. The hiking boot slipped right off.

"Oh, no." Piper paled, but she didn't make a move to retrieve his shoe.

Good. Ethan doubted Koko would willingly let it go. In any case, he didn't want it back.

The wolf knew.

It didn't make sense, but Ethan was convinced that was what was happening. Maybe it was some sort of animalistic sixth sense. Or maybe the wolf just recognized the scent of blood. And fear. And death. And grief. So much grief.

The wolf could have the shoes. Both of them.

Ethan pulled off his remaining hiking boot and tossed it to Koko. An offering to the ways of the wild.

"What are you doing?" Piper asked.

Ethan shrugged. "What am I going to do with just one shoe?"

"This is highly unusual. Koko doesn't make a practice of devouring shoes. Shasta maybe, but not Koko." Piper tore her attention away from the wolf and fixed her gaze with Ethan's. "Please believe me."

For the briefest of moments, looking into those earnest blue eyes of hers was almost like looking into a mirror. "I believe you."

She blinked. "You do?"

"Yes, I do." He believed. He believed in her passion. He believed in her commitment to the wolves. He believed that even though they were on opposite sides, he and Piper Quinn had something in common.

Something had happened in her past to make her identify with the wolves and care for them the way she did. She was their champion. A warrior. And warriors were seldom born. They were made. Ethan knew this all too well, because he was a warrior himself. He'd had his defining moment, and she'd had hers. Whatever had happened to her had cast her on the opposite path. The pendulum had swung the other direction. She couldn't walk away from the past any more than he could.

That didn't mean he would write the things she wanted him to write. He wished he could. Gazing into her looking-glass eyes, he wished it very much.

But he simply could not.

Chapter Two

The cursor on Ethan's laptop flashed on-off, on-off, taunting him. Daring him to write. He wasn't sure how long he'd been sitting at the Northern Lights Inn coffee bar, staring at his blank Word document. Definitely long enough to down several cups of coffee beneath the watchful eyes of the giant stuffed grizzly bear in the corner.

Ethan was less than fond of the bear. But given that it no longer possessed a heartbeat, he preferred it to Piper's wolves. Besides, he was in Alaska. Stuffed and mounted wildlife wasn't exactly an oddity. He couldn't even grocery shop at the corner store without rolling his cart past a moose head.

Even so, he'd chosen the seat farthest away from the bear. Unfortunately, that meant he was situated directly beneath an enormous bison head. Because, again, this was Alaska. He should have been grateful he wasn't given an antler to use as a stir stick.

He glared at the bison head. Bison were deadly. So deadly that they'd killed more people in Yellowstone National Park every year than bears had. Most people didn't know this. But Ethan knew.

Four years as a park ranger in Denali had taught him a

thing or two. But it had been a while since his park ranger days. A lot had happened. Too much. Five years was a long time, but it wasn't long enough to erase the sight of a little girl being torn apart by a bear. It wasn't long enough for him to forget the sounds of her screams. And it most definitely wasn't long enough to forget the remorse he'd felt at his failure to save her.

Of course, he probably could have sat beneath the mounted bison head without revisiting his past if he hadn't just spent the afternoon locked in a pen with a wolf.

He hadn't been ready to go home after leaving the wolf sanctuary. He wasn't sure why. If he thought hard enough about it, he'd probably realize that his reluctance to return to his quiet, empty house had something to do with the memories that had been unlocked by looking into the cool, dispassionate eyes of a wild animal. The scent of pine, the wind in his hair. The enigmatic Piper Quinn.

And his hiking boots. *The* hiking boots.

They'd been the shoes he'd worn the night of the bear mauling. They'd been at the back of his closet for years. When he'd left the park service in the wretched aftermath of the bear event, he'd traded cargo pants and hiking boots for more proper office attire. Knowing he'd likely be tramping through the forest today, he'd grabbed them and put them on this morning without thinking. Without remembering. And now everything had conspired to make him do just that. Remember.

The last place he wanted to be was someplace empty and quiet. Someplace like home. He needed distraction and conversation, and the Northern Lights Inn coffee bar was typically one of the busiest spots in Aurora. Which was why Ethan wasn't the least bit surprised when his friend Tate Hudson plopped down on the bar stool beside him, even though they'd had no plans to meet.

"Hey." Tate nodded at Ethan's blank screen. "Don't tell me you've got writer's block."

"Something like that." He clicked his laptop closed. Why was he having such difficulty writing this thing? The wolf sanctuary was a bad idea. The worst. Case closed. His article should be writing itself.

The wolves were an accident waiting to happen. He'd decided as much before he'd ever set eyes on Piper Quinn and her collection of sad rescue animals. Not that wolves typically preyed on humans. Ethan's rational self—the former park ranger that still lurked somewhere beneath his bruised and brooding surface—knew this.

Things happened in the wild. That's what *made* it wild. Just because wolves didn't make a habit of harming human beings didn't mean it would never come to pass. As Ethan saw it, the potential risk to the townspeople was reason enough for the wolf sanctuary to be shut down. And if it wasn't, he was certain the owners of the nearby reindeer farm would have an opinion on the matter. While the fair citizens of Aurora might not be on the typical wolf menu, reindeer most assuredly were. In recent years, the reindeer farm had become one of the town's most popular attractions. And its favorite resident was a certain reindeer named Palmer, who was something of an escape artist. Ethan ought to know. He'd penned his fair share of articles for the *Yukon Reporter* about Palmer's legendary antics. So this piece on the wolves should absolutely be writing itself. He wasn't sure why the words wouldn't come.

Tate ordered a plain black coffee and turned his attention back to Ethan. "You're starting to worry me, friend."

"Because I haven't finished my column?" He shrugged, even though his untouched Word document was starting to become cause for concern. He had a midnight deadline, after all.

"That—" Tate shot a bemused glance at Ethan's feet "—and the fact that you're sitting in a public place without shoes on your feet. In the dead of winter, I might add."

Ethan didn't feel like explaining his missing shoes any more than he felt like writing about them. Piper had given him a pair of silly-looking bedroom shoes so he wouldn't be forced to leave the sanctuary in his sock feet. He'd deposited them by the door of the hotel on his way in because he'd rather sit at the bar in his socks than too-small bunny slippers.

"Are you going to arrest me, Officer? Aren't you taking the whole 'no shirt, no shoes, no service' thing a bit far?" He looked pointedly at the shiny silver badge fixed to Tate's parka.

His friend shrugged. "I'll let it slide this time."

"Gee, thanks." Ethan stared into his empty coffee cup.

"Seriously, though. What gives with the socks?"

Ethan sighed. "I had a run-in with a wolf."

Tate's grin faded. "A wolf? Are you okay?"

Ethan pretended not to notice when his friend's gaze flitted briefly to the stuffed grizzly bear in the corner. Tate was one of the few people in Aurora who knew about what had happened in Denali. Since his work as a state trooper sometimes took him to other parts of Alaska, he'd known Ethan back then. Before. He was the only person Ethan still communicated with who'd been part of that world. He was a trusted friend. But that didn't mean Ethan wanted to have another heart-to-heart about his past.

He didn't want Tate's sympathy. He didn't want sympathy from anyone. He just wanted to write his piece and move on to something else. Another assignment. Something involving politics or sports. Or anything else he could write about without feeling as if he'd been emotionally eviscerated.

He gritted his teeth. "It wasn't like that."

The wolf had put an untimely end to his hiking boots, and Ethan had been a little rattled. That's all. Once his article was written, he'd forget all about Piper and her wolves and get on with his life.

Unless something happens to her.

"I'm doing a story on the new wolf sanctuary. Have you heard about it?"

Tate nodded. "A little. They just opened, right?"

"*She* just opened." *They* wasn't exactly accurate considering Piper's rescue center was essentially a one-woman show.

"She?" Tate's eyebrows rose. "Interesting."

"Anyhow, I'm fine." Ethan swallowed. "For the most part."

"If you say so." Tate studied him for a moment. Then, apparently convinced that Ethan wasn't on the verge of some kind of breakdown, he blew out a breath. "Try not to break any more laws, though."

Ethan slid him a sideways glance. "So going without shoes is, in fact, illegal?"

"Could be." Tate shrugged. "*Should* be, seeing as it's twenty degrees outside. Either way, just don't give me a reason to arrest you. I wouldn't want to have to take back the stellar job recommendation I gave you."

Ethan paused. Job recommendation? "*The Seattle Tribune*? You're kidding."

"Nope. Not kidding. They called me yesterday afternoon."

The Seattle Tribune. Finally. For almost a year now, Ethan had been applying for jobs at bigger newspapers. It was time to leave Alaska. Past time. But finding a newspaper job when print journalists were somewhat of a dying breed wasn't easy, especially given the fact that Ethan's only work experience was for a small regional paper.

His entire higher education had been designed to get him out of Manhattan and into the Land of the Midnight Sun. While his prep school friends had gone on to earn business or law degrees, Ethan had studied forestry and ecology, despite the overwhelming disapproval of his father. Ethan couldn't have cared less what his dad thought. Every move he'd made since he'd been old enough to formulate a plan had been designed to get him out of New York and into the wilds of Alaska. And he'd actually managed to do it.

For a time, life had been perfect. But then those wilds had gotten the better of him.

Of course, if he'd wanted to leave badly enough, he could have gone back to Manhattan. It's what his ex-wife had wanted. She'd begged him to leave Alaska and take the job his father had waiting for him in New York. Alaska had never been Susan's dream. She'd wanted to be a Madison Avenue wife and believed that once he'd gotten his Alaskan folly out of his system, they'd pack up and move back home.

Home.

New York had never felt like home. Not even when he was a kid. Growing up in his father's luxury hotel in the heart of Midtown, Ethan had had everything any boy could ever want. Except a backyard. Or a tree house. He'd spent the majority of his childhood indoors under the watchful eyes of the Pinnacle Hotel staff. He lived for outings to the park and rare weekends at the beach. He'd craved a place where he could see shooting stars at night and feel damp grass on his bare feet. Wide-open spaces where snow fell with a whisper of silence instead of the incessant cacophony of sirens and car horns.

In Alaska, he'd found the place of his dreams. Then in one tragic moment that dream had become a nightmare. The bear mauling changed Ethan. Or so Susan said when she'd packed her bags and gone back to Manhattan without him. Ethan didn't know what to believe. Not anymore.

"Yesterday? *The Seattle Tribune* called you yesterday, and you didn't think to mention it?"

"I'm mentioning it now, aren't I?" Tate drained his coffee cup and handed it to the barista for a refill. "Don't worry. I said only nice things about you, despite the fact that I think it's a mistake."

"It's not a mistake." It was a way to leave Alaska on his terms. Not his father's.

Of course, that was assuming Ethan got the job, which was an enormous assumption, considering he hadn't even been able to land a face-to-face interview. Yet. But this time they'd actually called his references. That had to be a good sign.

Tate swiveled to face him. "You belong here, Ethan. You always did, and you still do. Give it time, man."

Time.

Five years had already passed since the mauling in Denali, and it still felt as fresh as yesterday. He was beginning to give up on the notion that time healed all wounds.

"Can we not discuss this now?" Ethan ground out the words.

"Fine. But this isn't over. I'm not letting you pack up and move to the Lower 48 without having an actual conversation about it." Tate sighed, then mercifully changed the subject. "What's she like?"

"Who?" Ethan asked.

"The wolf woman."

Ethan paused. He'd been fully prepared to write the director of the Aurora Wolf and Wildlife Center off as hopelessly naive, or possibly even crazy. The drive from the *Yukon Reporter* offices to the thick forest of fir and aspen trees that covered the southern slope of the Chugach Mountains had been a long and winding one. There were moments when his SUV had hugged the edge of the cliff so closely that his speed didn't crawl above a cautious thirty miles per hour. The experience had afforded him plenty of opportunity to think about what kind of woman moved to a secluded spot halfway up a mountain with a pack of wolves.

But all the time in the world couldn't have prepared him for the reality of meeting Piper Quinn.

She was quite a bit younger than he'd expected. She couldn't be more than twenty-five, yet somehow she'd found the funding and ambition to open a thirty-five acre wildlife rescue center. He couldn't help but be impressed, despite the fact that he considered her project ill-advised at best, and at worst, just plain dangerous.

For starters, the sanctuary was too close to Aurora. The heart of the town was nestled right at the foot of the mountain. It might have been a slow crawl for an SUV, but an escaped wolf wouldn't need to travel the paved roads. A wolf could charge straight down the slope.

And then, while melted marshmallows had been dripping down his arm, she'd talked to him about saving species on the endangered list, the ecological importance of wolves and the National Nature Conservatory. Once upon a time, words such as those had been Ethan's vocabulary. He'd all but forgotten what it felt like to be passionate about nature, the bounty of the Alaskan wilderness and the beauty of creation. He'd forgotten pretty much everything, other than existing from day to day. And the things he would have given anything not to remember.

But he could see sparks of his former life in the fire that

burned in Piper Quinn's eyes. He got the feeling she'd done more living in her twenty-something years than most people did in a lifetime. She was smart. And she cared. Deeply.

What was she like? *Brilliant. Brave. Lovely.*

Something moved in Ethan. An ache. A different kind of ache than the hopeless regret that had become like a second skin. Different, but just as dangerous. Maybe even more so.

He swallowed. "She's interesting. Quite interesting, actually."

Not that it mattered.

Come morning, the lovely Piper Quinn was sure to despise him.

Piper didn't sleep a wink the night after Ethan Hale's visit. Instead she stayed up until all hours worrying about what he might write in his article. He'd been forced to leave the sanctuary in his sock feet, for goodness' sake. It was beyond mortifying. The man was probably suffering from frostbite now, and it was all her fault. She buried her head under her pillow, but it was no use. Not even a thick layer of goose down could keep the worry from finding its way into her thoughts.

Even the wolves seemed to sense that something was wrong. When Tundra let loose with a mournful howl right around midnight, the others didn't even bother chiming in. They were quiet, too quiet. Like the calm before a storm. A typewritten typhoon penned by Ethan Hale.

Sometime around one in the morning, she gave up the fight and made a batch of chocolate chip cookies. When that failed to make her drowsy enough to fall asleep, she whipped up a few dozen oatmeal raisin. Then molasses. By the time a misty violet dawn descended on the mountain, Piper couldn't tell if she was running a wildlife center or a bakery.

After checking on the wolves, she packed up the cookies and headed for the church. She would never manage to consume the fruits of her anxiety-fueled baking spree on her own, and she figured teenagers might be the only creatures walking the planet who were more ravenous than wolves. Besides, she owed the youth group a culinary thank-you for helping put up the fencing last week.

She pushed through the door of Aurora Community Church's fellowship hall with a nudge of her hip, her arms piled high with plastic bins.

"Piper, here. Let me help you." Liam Blake, the youth pastor, grabbed two containers from the top of her teetering stack.

His wife, Posy, a willowy ballerina who ran Aurora's one and only dance school and sometimes taught ballet at the church, snatched the rest. "Hi, Piper. What a surprise. What is all of this?"

"Cookies. Just a thank-you for the kids in the youth group." Arms free at last, Piper loosened the scarf around her neck and stomped the snow from her feet. Then she followed Posy and Liam to the youth pastor's office, where her Tupperware pretty much took up the entire surface of the desk.

So many cookies, so little sleep.

"This really wasn't necessary, although I'm sure they'll appreciate it." Liam opened one of the containers and popped a chocolate chip cookie in his mouth.

"If there are any left once school gets out," Posy teased.

"I couldn't plow my way through all of these if I tried." Liam laughed. "But I just might. They're delicious."

"Thanks. I'm glad you like them." Piper smiled. It was nice to have new friends. Different, but nice.

She was consciously aware of the fact that she spent the majority of her time with wolves. For the most part, she preferred it that way. Wolves were easier to understand than most people. Wolves had an organized, predictable social structure. You knew where you stood with wolves. Wolves didn't lie. And they didn't keep secrets.

Not that they were particularly noble. Like other animals, they were simply incapable of deception. What you saw was what you got. Their emotions showed clearly in their body language. Piper could tell if Koko was happy, sad, fearful or angry just by the way he carried his tail.

She'd often thought life would be so much simpler if the same could be said for people. It sure would have saved her the pain and heartache of getting involved with a man who specialized in secrets.

Piper's chest grew tight.

She didn't miss Stephen. She knew this now. Letting him go had been easy once she'd discovered the truth. Giving up on the idea of a home and a family—a *real* family— had cut closer to the bone.

She'd never had a family. The succession of foster homes where she'd grown up didn't count. Neither did the four brief years she'd lived with her birth mother. Was a mother really a mother when you could no longer remember her face, or her voice, or what it felt like to be held?

A child needed a mother. A home. Children needed structure. They needed to know where they fit in the world.

So did wolves. It was in their nature. That was one of the things Piper liked best about them. Every wolf had a place in the pack. Every wolf belonged. So eventually she'd become one of them, an honorary wolf. It was easier than trying to fit into the regular world. Most people thought wolves were dangerous, but those people hadn't grown up the way Piper had. Humans could be far more dangerous than wolves. And the damage they could do to a child's heart was immensely greater than bodily injury.

She should have known things would end badly with Stephen. She'd been so foolish to think she'd found a man who actually wanted to build a life with her and the wolves. She'd thought she had. He'd slipped an engagement ring on her finger, and she'd believed. She'd believed her pack would finally be complete. At last.

And then she'd found out that Stephen already belonged to a pack, complete with a wife and two children.

"How are things up in the mountains? Everything at the sanctuary running smoothly?" Liam asked, dragging Piper's attention back to the present.

Thank You, Lord.

She didn't like to dwell on the past, on Stephen's deception nor on her family. Most of the time, it didn't bother her that she lived a solitary life. Because she had the wolves, and they were like family. They were her world.

But her thoughts had begun to wander all over the place since yesterday. Since Ethan Hale.

"Great. Just great." She pasted on a smile. "At least I hope so."

"You hope so?" Posy glanced quickly at Liam and then back at Piper.

"I had a visitor yesterday—a journalist from the *Yukon Reporter.* He's doing a story on the sanctuary." She sank into one of the chairs beside Posy, opposite Liam's desk. Just thinking about the newspaper again hit her with a wave of exhaustion that made it difficult to stand up straight.

"Things didn't go well," Liam said. It was a statement, not a question. Piper was so preoccupied that she hardly noticed.

"It was a disaster. I just don't understand what happened. It was almost as though he'd made his mind up about the sanctuary before he'd even seen it." Yet there'd been a moment or two when she thought she'd spied a glimpse of a different Ethan Hale, a man who understood why she loved the wolves the way she did. Elusive, fleeting glances of a man with pine needles in his hair and the scent of wild things on his shoes instead of the gloomy journalist with storms in his eyes.

She swallowed around the lump that was quickly forming in her throat. "I'm worried about nothing. Maybe. Probably. I mean, surely things didn't go as badly as I think they did." She thought about mentioning Ethan's shoes, or lack thereof, but it was too mortifying to talk about.

Posy and Liam exchanged another glance.

The lump in Piper's throat grew three times larger. "Then again, perhaps I do have a reason to be worried."

She prayed with every fiber of her being that either Posy or Liam would say something reassuring.

Neither of them did.

"Actually, the article came out in this morning's paper. I have a copy of it right here." Posy bent to unzip the large black dance bag at her feet.

Piper felt sick as the woman extracted a copy of the *Yukon Reporter* and unfolded it to the proper page.

"Here." She handed it over.

Piper had to force herself to look at it.

Just rip it off. Like a Band-Aid.

She took a deep breath and started reading.

At first, things didn't seem so bad. Ethan wrote that her wolves had seemed obviously well cared for and that her dedication to their plight was admirable.

So far, so good. Piper allowed herself to breathe. Maybe this wasn't going to be as bad as she'd expected.

But then she read the next sentence, in which Ethan

called wolves predatory and carnivorous. Which was technically true. But he'd gone on to include an entire paragraph on wolf maulings without mentioning that such attacks were rare. So rare that Alaskans were infinitely more likely to be attacked by their family dog than a wolf.

Worse, he then pointed out that the sanctuary was inadequately staffed. The staff that she did have were legal minors who lacked the proper training to interact with wild animals.

Also technically true. But he'd made things sound so much worse than they actually were. The kids didn't interact with the wolves. They helped with things like fencing, preparing meat, landscaping and cleaning pens. Empty pens. She'd never allow one of the teens from the youth group to enter an enclosure without her close, personal supervision. She'd told Ethan as much.

This was bad. Really bad. Her panicked gaze flitted around the page, snagging on words like *clear and present danger*. Awful words. And apparently her wolves weren't just a threat to the people of Aurora. He mentioned the neighboring reindeer farm, as well.

That was the final straw. Piper sniffed, and the black newsprint swam before her eyes. She stopped reading, and an awkward, uncomfortable silence fell over the youth pastor's small office.

Not that Piper blamed the couple for going quiet. What were they supposed to say to the woman who'd apparently brought wolves to the area in order to ravage the townspeople and all of Santa's reindeer?

She hoped barefoot Ethan Hale *did* have frostbite. She hoped all ten of his toes fell off.

"We're so sorry, Piper," Posy said. "We were there. We saw the work that the kids did. We know they weren't any more in harm's way than if they'd been anywhere else out-doors in Alaska."

Liam leaned across his desk, his face so full of con-cern that it made Piper feel even worse. "What can we do to help?"

"I don't know." She shook her head. It was too late for help. The damage had been done. People all over Alaska were reading Ethan's damning words right this very min-ute. "I just can't believe it. This isn't even a news article. It's an attack on the sanctuary. It's full of opinions. Biased, inflammatory opinions with no basis in fact. I thought journalists were supposed to be impartial. He can't do this, can he? He just can't."

But he already had.

"It's an op-ed piece. That's why it's in the editorial sec-tion." Liam nodded at the top of the page, where *EDITO-RIAL* was printed in large block letters.

Piper blinked back a fresh wave of tears and glanced at the articles surrounding Ethan's piece on the sanctuary. "But I don't understand. Mine is the only negative article on this entire page."

"I know. I've actually never seen such a strongly worded piece in the *Yukon Reporter*." Posy turned toward Liam. "Have you?"

"Not that I recall," he said. "Something just doesn't seem right with this entire scenario."

Nothing was right about it. Absolutely nothing. "This will destroy me. People won't want to come see the wolves anymore. Not after this. And I can kiss my donations good-bye. Who in their right mind would want to give money to an organization that 'poses a clear and present danger to the community at large'?"

Nobody. That's who.

Beside her, Posy sighed. "Maybe it's not as bad as it

seems. It's an op-ed piece, as Liam said. By definition, that means it's an *opinion*. And this reporter is only one person."

"But he's one person with a voice that can reach the entire town. Folks know him. They respect him. Other than you two and the kids in the youth group, I don't really know people here. I'm new in town, remember?"

Posy's delicate eyebrows furrowed. "What you need is another voice, one to tell your side of the story. A voice that can explain why the wolves are important and why they aren't dangerous."

Liam nodded. "Posy's right. Maybe you can contact the editor and ask him to send another reporter out to the property. Actually, I know someone who used to work for the *Yukon Reporter*. Ben Grayson. He's a dog musher now, so he might be a little more sympathetic to your cause."

It was a kind offer, but it would take too long. Something needed to happen. Now. Before Ethan Hale's ill-formed opinion became accepted as truth. "You're right. What I need—what the *wolves* need—is another voice."

"Do you want me to give Ben Grayson a call?" Liam reached for his phone.

Piper lifted her chin. She'd driven all the way from Colorado to Alaska with a trailerful of wolves. She'd put the sanctuary together from the ground up. She could do this. "Thank you, but no. After this fiasco, there's only one person I trust to tell my side of the story."

Liam set his phone down. "Who?"

"Me." It was the perfect solution. Who was she kidding? It was the *only* solution. "I'm going to write the article myself."

Chapter Three

The morning after his op-ed piece on the wolf sanctuary appeared in the *Yukon Reporter*, Ethan began his day as he always did. He got ready for work, then drove the twenty miles from his cabin near Knik all the way back to the coffee bar at the Northern Lights Inn. Aurora was in the opposite direction of his office, which meant he was spending an extra half hour or so in his car just for coffee. But it was worth it. The coffee at the Northern Lights was *that* good.

Besides, he was up earlier than usual. He hadn't exactly gotten a good night's sleep after he'd finally turned in his article.

"Morning, Ethan." The barista slid a coaster across the smooth walnut surface of the bar and grinned. "What can I get you this morning?"

"A large Gold Rush blend. Black, please," Ethan said. "Thanks."

"Sure thing." The barista smiled again. Either Ethan was imagining things or Sam seemed more outwardly cheerful than usual.

"So everyone in Aurora is talking about your article.

You know…the one about the wolves." Sam eyed him over the top of the espresso machine.

The one about the wolves. It had to be that one? Couldn't they talk about the piece he'd written about the upcoming city elections or the one about Arctic ice melt season?

"Is that right?" Ethan shifted on his bar stool.

He shouldn't feel uncomfortable about what he'd written. He absolutely shouldn't. He'd been doing his job. That was all. His extensive knowledge of Alaskan ecology and wildlife was one of the reasons he'd landed his job at the paper in the first place. They'd asked him to write an educated opinion on the wolf sanctuary, and he'd complied.

He'd done the right thing. The safe thing. The town would be better off without the wolves. So would Piper Quinn. She just didn't know it.

"Oh, yes." Sam let out a laugh. "Your article already caused quite a stir around here, and now this morning—"

Ethan's cell phone rang, cutting the barista off.

It was just as well. Ethan may have had no reason to feel bad about what he'd written, but that didn't mean he wanted to discuss it with Sam. Or with Tate, who'd left a few voice mails the day before.

Ethan couldn't keep avoiding his closest friend. Tate probably wanted to make sure he was okay after losing his shoes to a wild animal. There had been an underlying note of concern in his voice in the messages he'd left.

That hint of worry was exactly why Ethan had been reluctant to return his calls. Couldn't he leave the past dead and buried, where it belonged?

Dead.

Buried.

Ethan's temples throbbed. He glanced at the display on his phone, expecting to see Tate's name. It wasn't. LOU MARSHALL. His editor. "Hello, Lou."

"Ethan, I'm glad you picked up. I need you to get into the office early today." He sounded urgent. Even more urgent than he usually did, which was extremely urgent. He was, after all, a newsman.

"How early?"

"As soon as you can get here. We need to talk about this wolf woman. Immediately. Just get here."

The line went dead.

We need to talk about this wolf woman.

Super.

Ethan sighed. "Sam, I'm going to need that coffee to go."

Half an hour later, after breaking as few traffic laws as possible, he plunked two cups of Gold Rush blend down on Lou Marshall's desk and pushed one toward his boss. "Morning. You said we needed to talk?"

Lou took a gulp of coffee and nodded. "Yes. Have you seen the paper yet this morning?"

"No. I just got here." He frowned at the copy of the *Yukon Reporter* early edition in Lou's hands and remembered Sam's line of questioning at the coffee bar. "Has there been a new development in the wolf story?"

"You could say that." Lou tossed the newspaper at him.

Ethan caught it with one hand.

He died a thousand deaths in the handful of seconds it took for him to find the "development" that Lou had referred to. A thousand deaths in which he imagined every potential tragedy, every conceivable fatal accident that could have taken place. Escaped wolves. Wounded people.

Not her. God, please. Not her.

The hasty prayer caught him nearly as off guard as Piper's letter to the editor on page three. Ethan couldn't remember the last time he'd prayed. Actually, he could. It had been on a cold Denali night five years ago when the world had fallen apart. He'd screamed to the heavens that night as he'd tried in vain to put it back together, mistakenly believing that there was a God somewhere up there who listened. Who cared.

He stared at the letter, and the panic that had caught him in its grip morphed into irritation. Piper hadn't been hurt. She was perfectly fine. So fine that she'd been busy writing a letter to his boss. And Lou had *printed it in the paper*.

"You've got to be kidding," Ethan muttered, scanning the contents as quickly as his gaze could move over the page, catching glimpses of words such as *yellow journalism*, *unfair reporting* and *retraction*.

Blood boiling, he wadded the paper into a ball and pitched it into the trash. *Retraction?* She wanted him to take his words back? Out of the question. "If you've called me in here to demand that I print a retraction, you're wasting your breath. I won't do it."

"I wouldn't dream of making such a demand." A smile creased Lou's face and he calmly raised his coffee cup to his mouth again.

Then what was Ethan doing here? He was almost afraid to ask.

As it turned out, he had reason to be afraid. "On the contrary, I want you to write whatever you like about Ms. Quinn and her wolves. Repeatedly. The paper is sold out all over the state. This wolf thing is moving papers faster than we can print them. I want you to keep writing about the wolves, provided you do so on location."

Ethan froze while reaching for his coffee. "On location?"

"Yes. On location. I've already arranged everything. You're to spend the next two weeks volunteering at the Aurora Wolf and Wildlife Center alongside Ms. Quinn. You'll document the experience in a daily diary that will run on the front page of the *Yukon Reporter*." Lou slung back the final dregs of his coffee. "It's genius, don't you think?"

Volunteer at the wolf sanctuary? For *two weeks*? With wolves?

With Piper?

Ethan had plenty of thoughts on the idea. Genius was nowhere on the list.

"No." His temples throbbed harder. The notion of facing Piper after the things he'd written about her—not to mention the things that *she'd* written about *him*—was enough to give him an aneurysm. "Just…no."

"You heard me say that your daily diary will run on the front page, right?" Lou waggled his eyebrows.

"Why? I've been asking you for a spot on the front page for months." That was an understatement. He was certain it had been a regular topic of conversation for the better part of a year. "Why now? Why this?"

"Because the readers are eating it up." Lou threw up his hands and laughed. "Since her response to your op-ed came out this morning, the phone hasn't stopped ringing. People love it. You and Piper Quinn are all that anyone in Alaska can talk about."

This cannot be happening. Ethan was supposed to write the article. Piper was supposed to close her doors, and that would be the end of it.

He should have known she wouldn't give up this easily.

He breathed out a sigh. "But I don't want people talking about Piper and me. Not in the same breath, anyway."

"Too late. Just do a Google search of yourself. The first two screens are chock-full of results about the war of words between you and the wolf woman."

A Google search? "No, thank you."

Lou shrugged. "Suit yourself, but get packing. I've already made a reservation for you at the Northern Lights Inn. That way, you can spend as much time as possible on the property."

At least he'd be in close proximity to great coffee. *If* he agreed to this nonsensical plan, which he wouldn't.

He shook his head. "No."

"The front page, Ethan. It's all yours. Every day, for fourteen days straight." Lou tapped a finger on the newspaper that lay on the desk between them.

The front page.

For two solid weeks.

If that didn't get the attention of *The Seattle Tribune*, nothing would. It was a reporter's dream. *His* dream.

Then why did it feel so much like a nightmare? "Where on the front page?"

"Bottom right-hand corner. Twenty inches of space per day."

"Above the fold. Twenty-*five* inches." If Ethan was going to agree to this nonsense, he would make sure it was worth his while.

"Deal." Lou slapped his hand on the desk in triumph. The coffee cups jumped in time with the throbbing of Ethan's headache. "You'd better get packing. The clock is ticking. Your first diary entry is due no later than midnight tonight. Ms. Quinn is expecting you."

Piper was expecting him.

What have I done?

"Get cracking, son." Lou shooed Ethan out of his office. "And don't look so worried. This is going to be the highlight of your career. Think of it as being embedded, like a reporter in a combat zone."

A reporter in a combat zone.

Why did Ethan get the feeling that the comparison wasn't too far off the mark?

* * *

Piper was ready and waiting when she heard the tires of Ethan's SUV roll up the sanctuary's snow-covered drive. She closed the field notebook where she recorded daily observations about each wolf's behavior patterns, climbed down from the large flat boulder overlooking the property and was standing, arms crossed, toe tapping, by the time her nemesis-turned-volunteer climbed out of his car.

"You're late," she said by way of greeting. She wasn't wasting her time with marshmallows and small talk this time. A fat lot of good that had done.

"Piper." He nodded. "We meet again."

He looked as stone-faced as ever, which pretty much confirmed that he hadn't lost one minute of sleep over the hurtful things he'd written about her. Not just her, but the wolves, the sanctuary, her goals and dreams. Basically, everything she held near and dear.

Unbelievable.

The email she'd received the night before from Lou Marshall at the *Yukon Reporter* had been nothing if not concise. He'd received her letter and would be printing it in the early edition. No apology. No retraction. But her letter would appear in the paper. She'd been appeased. For the most part.

And then the impossible had happened. Only a few hours after the early edition of the paper had been released, Lou Marshall had called and asked if she'd be interested in Ethan volunteering at the sanctuary for two weeks and chronicling the experience in the newspaper. Of course she'd said yes. Another article from a different perspective was exactly what she'd demanded. What Marshall was offering her was above and beyond that. Fourteen articles. Plus two weeks of free labor.

It was an offer she couldn't refuse, even if it did mean

spending approximately eighty hours in the presence of the self-righteous Ethan Hale. As much as she hated to admit it, she could use the help. Especially help from someone as physically strong and capable as Ethan appeared. There were plenty of chores around the sanctuary that required an able body. Just yesterday poor wiry Caleb had nearly collapsed under the weight of a cord of firewood.

Not that she'd noticed Ethan's broad chest. Or strapping shoulders. Or thick, muscular forearms.

Okay, so maybe she'd noticed those things, as well as his other knee-weakening qualities. Such as the way his piercing gray eyes looked almost blue beneath the shelter of the hemlock trees. And the way he somehow seemed at home here among the woods and the rocks and the snow flurries. Like the wolves—untamable, yet not wholly wild.

It was a ridiculous notion. He didn't deserve to be compared to her beloved wolves, even in the secrecy of her thoughts. Because those arms, those shoulders and those extraordinary lupine eyes were all attached to his impossibly stubborn head.

She looked up at him now, towering over her with his chiseled features arranged in an expression of distinct displeasure. He shifted his weight from one foot to the other, obviously longing to be someplace else. *Anyplace* else but here.

What was I thinking, agreeing to this? It's a terrible idea.

After getting the phone call from his editor, she'd actually wondered if maybe the arrangement had been Ethan's idea. That maybe, just maybe, he regretted dragging her name through the mud in one of Alaska's biggest media outlets. Perhaps he'd felt remorseful after he'd read her response in her letter to the editor.

Judging by the look on his face, clearly not.

She swallowed. This could be a mistake. And she couldn't afford another mistake. But really, what else could he write that could make things worse?

Mistake or not, if he thought she was going to bend over backward in welcome again, he had another think coming. She wasn't the only one making mistakes lately. Ethan had underestimated her before. He hadn't taken her at all seriously. That was a mistake she aimed to fix.

She crossed her arms again and pinned him with a stare. "I repeat—you're late."

She had a tour arriving in less than ten minutes. How was she supposed to get him properly trained to do anything of any value while she was lecturing her guests and showing them around? Over half her scheduled visitors had either canceled or no-showed so far today, thanks to him. Those who still wanted to see the wolves were getting the royal treatment.

"Your editor told me to expect you nearly an hour ago."

"My apologies." His mouth curved in an obviously disingenuous grin. "I had a pressing errand to run on the way here."

"And what might that have been?" Had he stopped to picket the local animal shelter or something? Had he been busy kicking puppies?

He crossed his massive arms. Honestly, how did a man with a desk job end up with such nice biceps? "If you must know, I had to stop and buy new shoes."

She glanced down at his feet, clad in a pristine pair of North Face all-weather hiking boots, and her cheeks grew warm. "Oh. I see."

"So am I forgiven?" He lifted a single, bemused brow.

"For the tardiness, yes. For everything else, no. Not even close."

"I can live with that. Somehow."

Could he be any more smug? "I honestly don't know how you manage to sleep at night."

"I manage." He shrugged, then his gaze fell on her notebook. "What's that you have there?"

"My field notes." She held the book tighter to her chest. "A written record of the daily behavior patterns of my subject. In this case, the wolves."

"I know what a field notebook is. Does that surprise you?" He planted his hands on his hips, and Piper vowed not to look at his arms again.

Half a second later, her gaze zeroed in on his forearms. She cleared her throat. "Actually, it does surprise me. Quite a bit."

"May I have a look?" he asked, gesturing to her notebook.

"Certainly." She offered it to him. Maybe if he realized how seriously she took her work with the wolves, he'd relent and give her at least an ounce of respect.

He flipped through the pages and glanced up only when he'd reached the end. "Impressive."

"Thank you." Heat rose to her cheeks. One kind word from Ethan Hale, wolf hater extraordinaire, and she was blushing like a schoolgirl. She'd never hated herself more in her entire life.

"Is this part of your paperwork for the NNC grant?"

"Yes, it is." How in the world could he possibly know that? Why would he be familiar with NNC grant requirements?

"I see," he said, cryptic as always. Good grief, he could be annoying.

She held out her hand. "Now give it back, please. I have a tour to conduct, and you have work to do."

Field notes back in hand, she turned, stomped through the snow toward the wheelbarrow that was propped beside the log cabin, and wheeled it back toward him to park it at his immaculate feet.

He eyed it with trepidation. "What's this?"

"It's your first assignment." She smiled. She was enjoying herself. Too much, probably. But she couldn't help it. "I'd like you to clean up Tundra's enclosure. The pitchfork is leaning against the fence. And don't worry. I've relocated her to a different pen for the time being so you can move about without fear of being eaten alive."

A muscle twitched in his jaw. "You want me to clean a wolf pen."

"No." She shook her head. "I want you to clean *all* the wolf pens."

Ethan narrowed his gaze and released a controlled breath. "All of them?"

"They're not going to clean themselves, are they?" She was fully aware he would write about this. And she didn't care. Anyone who'd read his less-than-flattering portrayal of her life's work would understand. "Start with Tundra's enclosure. Just remove the dirty straw and replace it with fresh. New bales are piled behind the cabin. Your main job is to remove all of the soiled material."

"Soiled material," he repeated. He didn't sound the least bit amused anymore. In fact, he sounded angry.

Good.

"I'm referring to animal waste." She smiled sweetly.

He glared at her. Hard. "Believe me. I know exactly what you're referring to, Piper."

"Excellent. I'm so glad we understand one another."
Since we're going to be spending so much time together...

The flicker in his gaze told her that he was thinking about the same thing she was—hours, days, *weeks* in one another's company. She already felt distinctly ill at ease after little more than three minutes.

"Piper..." His voice grew soft, almost tender.

If she listened closely, she could almost hear an unspoken apology. Almost.

She wanted to tell him not to bother. It was too little, too late. The damage had been done. Words had created this mess. Words could fix it...*maybe*...but those words were going to have to be addressed to a bigger audience.

Besides, she didn't like hearing him say her name like that, as if he knew her. As if he cared. It was confusing. And she'd had more than enough confusion in her life.

"I think it's best that you go back to calling me Ms. Quinn, since you're working here now." Maybe she was pouring it on a little thick. Then again, maybe not.

Ethan's gaze hardened. "Is that what the kid calls you?" He jerked his head toward Caleb, who was busy filling water buckets. "He works here, too, doesn't he?"

Ethan sounded almost jealous, which was just plain ludicrous. Almost as ludicrous as the way his potential jealousy made her feel all warm inside, despite the snow flurries enveloping them both.

She squared her shoulders. "Caleb calls me Piper. And yes, he works here. But he's also managed to refrain from slandering me to the greater Alaskan population."

She glanced down at the wheelbarrow, then at Ethan's shiny new boots. Footwear that would likely be unrecognizable by the end of the day. He'd probably also acquire a blister or two. Such a pity.

She beamed up at him. "Enjoy yourself. I have a tour to give."

Ethan stood seething as Piper strode through the snow toward a small group that had assembled by the log cabin headquarters while they'd been exchanging pleasantries.

Not that their interaction had been entirely pleasant. Or pleasant at all, for that matter.

He wasn't an idiot. He'd expected Piper to be angry. Just not quite this angry.

He had a diary entry to write at the end of the day. No, not a diary entry. A newspaper article. For all practical purposes, she'd just demanded that he spend the afternoon cleaning a thirty-five-acre litter box. If she thought he wouldn't write about this, she was fooling herself. How exactly did she expect to gain the respect of his readership when she was behaving this way?

More importantly, how was he supposed to write eight hundred words about such a repugnant task?

Ethan pressed the heels of his palms against his eyes. He'd been nursing a headache since the moment Lou had dumped this crazy assignment on him. Ethan was embedded all right. And now that he'd arrived in enemy territory, the pounding behind his eyes had intensified tenfold.

He huffed out a breath. He needed to forget about trying to write something riveting about cleaning up wolf pens. He just needed to report the sloppy truth. And he *really* needed to stop worrying about how that truth would make Piper look. Let her shoot herself in the foot. At least her public humiliation wouldn't be his fault. This time.

He grabbed the handles of the wheelbarrow and aimed it in the direction of the enclosure. The first gate to the pen stood propped open with a pitchfork. Ethan took it, gripping the handle a little too tightly as he unlatched the second gate and stepped inside. His gaze swept the snow-covered ground, the pale bark of the aspen trees and the silver slate rocks that punctuated the landscape. So much white.

The memory of Tundra's snowy coat crept into his consciousness. His throat grew tight, and he searched the area for a glimpse of lupine copper eyes. Just in case.

Get on with things. The wolf's not here.

He thrust the pitchfork into a pile of snow near the fence and went back for the wheelbarrow. As he maneuvered it inside, the gate slammed shut behind him with a clang of finality. Ethan reached again for the pitchfork. If he didn't get started, he'd be here all night. But before his hand made contact, he heard a rustling in the distance.

He paused.

And waited.

Just when he'd convinced himself that he'd been hearing things, a twig snapped somewhere behind the tree line. His head jerked in the direction of the noise. Another memory washed over him. Not so much a single recollection as a collection of sensations—a stirring in the alder thickets, a dizzying brown blur exploding from the brush, an up-turned basket of wild blueberries, the hot breath of the bear on his neck, then the sticky sweet smell of blood. Ethan's hands balled into fists, his body preparing for battle as he fought against the pictures in his head.

A breeze blew through the enclosure, sending snow tumbling from the boughs of the evergreens. It fell like a heavy, frozen curtain. Ethan saw nothing but white. He blinked against the assault, eyes stinging in the Arctic wind. Shaken by his memories, he couldn't be certain what was real and what wasn't. Had he really heard a creature in the enclosure? Was the ghostly shape he thought he saw moving among the trees really the elusive white wolf, Tundra, or was his tortured mind playing tricks on him?

His answer came in the form of a tiny white fluff ball that hopped out from between two hemlocks. A rabbit. Specifically, a snowshoe hare with a winter-white pelt and dark, watchful eyes. It blinked at him, twitched its quivering nose and hopped out of view.

Ethan released the breath he hadn't even realized he'd been holding. He felt off-kilter, dizzy. He'd been completely unnerved.

By a bunny.

He glanced over his shoulder in search of Piper. Relief swept over him when he spotted her in the distance, surrounded by a small group of people wearing puffy coats, mittens and rapt expressions. He wondered what she was saying that had them so enamored. Not that it mattered. He was going to be around for a while. Days. Weeks. He'd hear her spiel eventually. In the meantime, he should just say a silent prayer of thanks that she hadn't witnessed his moment of panic.

Her words from three days ago came back to him.

While wolves are indeed predators, I wouldn't be so quick to call them dangerous...unless you're a bunny rabbit.

The sentiment, which he'd merely found annoying at the time, now seemed prophetic. Uncomfortably so. Because in his wildest dreams, he'd never imagined that he himself would be the bunny rabbit in this scenario.

He was afraid.

Of what, he wasn't even sure. It wasn't the wolves. His feelings were more complicated than that. It was his past, the memories, the wolves and nature itself all rolled together in a tangle of anger, regret, dread...and loss. Loss of life. Loss of control.

So much loss.

He was broken. Broken and bitter. That much he'd known. But he hadn't realized that his fury was also suffused with fear. It was a sobering realization. The wind, the snow, the slender pine boughs were all things he'd once loved. Before the bear attack, he'd slept outside during the summer months, under the stars, more often than he'd lain in a bed at night. That's why he'd come to Alaska all those years ago. He'd wanted to a build a life in the most majestic place on earth. The kid who'd spent his childhood with his face pressed against hotel windows had beaten a trail to the Last Frontier as quickly as he could.

Where had that fearless soul gone?

Ethan stabbed at a pile of straw with the pitchfork and heaved it into the wheelbarrow. Then he did the same thing again, and again. With each jab, he felt the muscles in his arms and back loosen, then begin to burn. But it was a good burn, the kind of sharp ache that came with physical work.

He made short work of cleaning out Tundra's pen. Piper seemed genuinely surprised, and possibly even a little impressed, when he told her he was ready to move on to the next enclosure. She even smiled as she escorted Tundra back to her pen. And the way she did was altogether different from the sassy grin she'd greeted him with earlier. This was a genuine smile, full of sweetness and light. Looking at it brought about an ache in the center of his chest that made him forget the burn in his biceps.

But Ethan knew better. The smile was for the wolf. Not for him. What he didn't know was why it made him feel so empty inside.

Chapter Four

"Is this true?" Posy lowered the morning edition of the *Yukon Reporter* and, mouth agape, stared at Piper. "Did you really make him clean out the wolf pens?"

Piper swallowed. "He put that in his article?"

"Yes. It says so right here." Posy tapped the front page with her index finger.

Piper hadn't been able to bring herself to read Ethan's account of his first day volunteering at the sanctuary, even though procuring a copy of the newspaper was precisely why she'd driven into town.

That had been the plan, anyway, when she'd headed down the mountain. She'd intended to grab a newspaper at the corner store and then head right back up. Instead, she'd found herself at the church with three coffees in tow—hers, plus one each for Liam and Posy. The church had been quiet, though. The parking lot had been empty and the doors locked.

She should have headed straight back to the wildlife sanctuary. She had work to do. Loads of it. But when she'd driven past Posy's ballet school and seen the warm glow of light through its windows, her car had somehow parked itself in the closest parking space.

She liked Posy. Posy was the closest thing to a friend she had here, so it was only natural that Piper should stop by and say good morning. She wasn't putting off going back to the sanctuary because she was nervous about being alone with Ethan. He had nothing to do with it.

Well, maybe a little. Just a tad.

"He wrote all about it." Posy pulled a face. "In excruciating detail, I might add."

Piper shrugged. "It's a dirty job, but somebody's got to do it." *And that somebody may as well be Ethan.*

Posy narrowed her gaze at Piper over the rim of her coffee cup. "I thought the point of having him write these articles was for the community to see the wolf sanctuary in a more positive light."

"It is." A small knot of something that felt too much like guilt settled in Piper's stomach. She had nothing to feel guilty about. If anyone should be tormented by remorse, it was Ethan. He should be racked with guilt day and night over what he'd done.

Okay, so maybe that would be extreme. Then again, maybe not.

She turned the newspaper facedown on Posy's desk so she wouldn't have to see Ethan's penetrating gaze staring back at her from the thumbnail photo above his byline. It was altogether distracting. "All I want is for people to support the sanctuary and appreciate the wolves."

"Are you sure that's *all* you want?" Posy's lips quirked into a grin that she apparently couldn't hold back any longer.

Busted.

So maybe Piper wanted some retribution. Just the tiniest possible amount. She was only human, after all. "Point taken. Revenge will get me nowhere. Plus it's wrong. I'll give Ethan something less…messy to do today."

She'd do just that as soon as she got to the sanctuary. Of course, who knew when exactly that would be, since she apparently wasn't in any hurry to get there.

Caleb's mother had called Piper late the night before to tell her that he'd come down with a nasty stomach bug. He wouldn't be around as a buffer. It would be her and Ethan. Just the two of them. Alone.

Except for the wolves.

She should get going. Ethan was probably roaming around the sanctuary right now, wondering where she was. If only he didn't look so ruggedly handsome while he did so. Then maybe, just maybe, the thought of working in tandem with him wouldn't make her feel so uncomfortable.

A nervous flutter passed through her. *Get a grip. You can't hide in the ballet studio until school gets out.* She ordered herself to stand and go, but her backside stubbornly remained planted in the chair opposite Posy's desk. Since when had she turned into the kind of woman who hid from a little meaningless confrontation?

Since that confrontation had somehow become meaningful.

She pushed that thought away and watched Posy slip her feet into a pair of soft pink ballet slippers.

"You're welcome to stay and watch my baby ballerina class if you like," she said, rising from her chair and moving into a series of deep knee bends.

Piper blinked. "Baby ballerinas? You mean babies, as in infants?"

"Sorry." Posy laughed. "Not actual babies. Four-year-olds. As far as ballet goes, they're babies."

"That's actually impressive. I'm surprised four-year-olds can even do ballet." Not that Piper could stay and watch. That would be taking her avoidance of Ethan to a whole new level.

"They can plié. And they love to glissade." Posy noticed what was surely the blank look on Piper's face. "That means gliding."

"Of course it does." Piper grinned. "Maybe I need to sign up for baby ballet. It sounds like I could learn a few things."

Posy laughed. "You don't quite fit the age requirements, but since opening this place has cost Liam and me a small fortune, I might be persuaded to make an exception. I could use a new student. Or twelve. You'd be the tallest in the class. You could be the tree in the center of our forest."

"There's a forest?" Piper looked around the pristine studio, with its mirrored walls and smooth wood floor, and tried to imagine a cluster of aspen and paper birch trees taking root.

"Well, for right now it's only imaginary. I'm having the girls pretend that the wind is blowing their arms out and they have to tiptoe through the trees. We have a recital coming up next month, and it would be great if the baby ballerina class could participate. I just have to come up with a story of some sort. A story that could be told with very simple steps and inexpensive costumes."

"In a pretend forest." Suddenly caring for a ragtag pack of rescued wolves didn't seem all that difficult.

"Right." Posy grimaced. "Surely I can come up with something. The older girls are doing *Cinderella* and *Snow White*. There's got to be something for the little ones to do. They look so cute in their tiny ballet shoes. I know their parents would love to see them dance. The rest of the town, too, possibly."

Cinderella and *Snow White*, the quintessential fairytale princesses. Of course, Piper's tastes ran more along the lines of *Little Red Riding Hood*. That story had everything—wind, a forest, trees.

A wolf.

Piper grew very still in her chair, her coffee cup midway to her mouth. But her thoughts were suddenly spinning out of control. She could already see it—Posy's youngest students tiptoeing across the floor in bright red tutus and capes, papier-mâché trees rising up from the floor and green tissue paper leaves hanging from the ceiling. Dim lights, whimsical music and a wolf, a *real* wolf. One of Piper's wolves.

Koko could do it. In Colorado, she'd taken him on at least half a dozen school visits. At a year and a half, he hadn't yet developed enough adult wolf tendencies to be standoffish around people. Adolescent wolves were almost like puppies. They were interested. Curious. But most wolves were easily spooked by strange people and new places.

Koko was unique. He didn't get stressed around crowds, so long as the atmosphere was calm. He'd grown up on a photo farm, bred and born to look cute in pictures for calendars, T-shirts and coffee mugs. As a tiny wolf pup, he'd been handled constantly.

Then he'd outgrown his cuteness, and things had taken a turn for the worse.

He was too big. Too imposing. Too wolfish. So he'd been abandoned, left in a Dumpster to starve. He was barely found in time. Then the hands that touched him no longer belonged to people he knew from the farm, but rather to strangers. Veterinarians. Medical professionals.

Piper felt sick every time she thought about what had happened to Koko, but at least he was safe now. And his constant exposure to human interaction made him an ideal ambassador for his species. He was accustomed to people. He could even walk on a leash. She could bring him onstage, on a lead, near the end of the dance.

It would be adorable. The townspeople would love it.

Best of all, it would draw a huge amount of attention to both the ballet school and the wolf sanctuary. Posy had just mentioned that the school was struggling. She could use some new students. And the rescued wolves could use all the positive attention they could get.

It would be perfect.

Wouldn't it?

Of course Piper thought it was a precious idea. But Posy might think she'd lost her mind. Ethan most certainly would.

This has nothing whatsoever to do with that man.

With one notable exception. Along with being a great public relations opportunity for the ballet school and the wolf sanctuary, helping out with Posy's recital would give Piper something to think about other than Ethan Hale.

Her gaze met Posy's and held. "I might have an idea."

Ethan didn't intend to get to the wolf sanctuary a full hour before Piper expected him. He didn't aim to get there early at all, lest she mistakenly think her reprimand for his tardiness the day before carried any weight whatsoever. He'd planned on arriving right at eight-thirty. No earlier, no later.

But at six in the morning, the very minute the early edition of the *Yukon Reporter* hit newsstands, his cell phone had begun ringing. An hour and a half later, it still hadn't stopped.

He'd resorted to putting it on vibrate so he could have a moment of peace as he drove to the wolf sanctuary. He needed a minute—or ten—to collect himself before he embarked on another day as Piper Quinn's assistant.

Assistant. Right. Slave labor was a more accurate description. He'd tossed and turned more than once during the night, wondering what delightful task she had in store for him today. Worry. Anxiety. Dread. Those had to be the reasons for his sleeplessness. He refused to believe it had anything to do with the fact that every time he closed his eyes, he saw Piper's exquisite face, sapphire eyes sparkling with life, her flaxen hair whipping in the wind. She had such an animated spirit that even the air around her refused to stand still. Snow flurries danced. The boughs of the evergreens waved as she walked past. It was as if nature were every bit as enamored with her as she was with it.

Not Ethan. He was irritated, not enamored. Not by any stretch. Definitely irritated. Possibly intrigued. But that's where his feelings stopped, sleepless nights notwithstanding.

He scowled at his phone buzzing away in the cup holder of his SUV. Lou had already called three times, as had pretty much every columnist and reporter at the office. Ethan had never been on the receiving end of so much effusive praise.

He should be happy. His work was getting the sort of attention he'd wanted since he'd given up his park ranger days for a cubicle in a newsroom. Correction: this was the *amount* of attention he'd wished for. The *nature* of the accolades was another story.

His column wasn't newsworthy. It was scandalous. The feud between the "reporter and the wolf lady" was suddenly all that the people of Aurora were talking about it. According to Lou, it was on the tip of every tongue in the Land of the Midnight Sun, from the frozen shores of the Chukchi Sea to Sitka, near the southernmost tip of the state. Ethan's newspaper account of his first day on the job had only added fuel to the fire.

Readers were thrilled. Lou was thrilled. Ethan *should* have been thrilled.

He wasn't. Not quite. Because it had suddenly occurred to him that he was no longer writing the news. He *was* the news. And that didn't sit well.

Even worse, he should have seen this coming. He should have realized that instead of signing on to write a series of articles about a dangerous situation that posed a threat to the community, he'd actually agreed to pen what amounted to a gossip column. About himself, no less.

All the red flags had been there. They still were. When he'd sat down at the Northern Lights Inn coffee bar earlier this morning, every pair of eyes in the place had been on him. Every customer had asked him about Piper. And her wolves. And what she might have in store for him next, now that he'd cleaned out the wolf enclosures. Even the barista had peppered him with inquiries before handing over Ethan's coffee. He'd stood on the other side of the counter holding the large paper cup of Gold Rush blend hostage until Ethan had finally answered one of his questions. Questions that had nothing to do with the ecological and social realities of the wolf sanctuary, but everything to do with his plans to get even with Piper. And vice versa.

What had he done? Maybe he should pull the plug on this whole thing and tell Lou he was finished.

Right. And then Lou would fire him on the spot.

Ethan swallowed the dregs of his coffee as he maneuvered his SUV off the highway and onto the snow-covered road that led to the wolf sanctuary. Maybe there was a way to salvage this situation, to draw attention to the actual matter at hand—the danger that the wolves posed—rather than the "war" between him and Piper. Ethan was a man of words. Granted, his words of late hadn't been pretty. But *war* was an ugly word. The ugliest of all.

They weren't at war, were they?

He hoped not. He liked Piper. More than he had any reason to. More than he should.

The sanctuary certainly didn't look like a battlefield. Through the softly falling snow, beneath the thick canopy of the evergreens, it looked more like something from a Christmas card. Peaceful. Serene.

And just a little bit lonely.

There was no sign of the beat-up old VW van that was usually parked out front, and no sign of Piper. He wondered where on earth she could have gone at this early hour, then reminded himself it was none of his business. She wasn't expecting him until eight-thirty.

He switched off the ignition and was struck by the sudden silence. Silence so thick that it was heavy, like a weight on his chest. Out here, it was easy to forget that downtown Aurora was little more than ten miles away. The forest was a different world, among trees and rugged stone cliffs. Among the wolves.

Ethan frowned. He didn't like the idea of Piper living out here all alone. What if one of the wolves turned on her? No one would be around to help.

Wolf attacks on humans were rare. Piper was right about that. But there was a big difference between rare and impossible. Only three people in North America had been killed by wolves in the past fifty years, but the most recent attack had been right in Piper's backyard. Less than five years ago.

A schoolteacher out for a late-afternoon jog near Chignik Lake, Alaska, was attacked and killed by a pack of wild wolves. She'd been less than two miles from a small but populated village, closer to civilization than Piper's sanctuary. Like Piper, the victim had been a woman. Petite, blonde, beautiful.

Gone.

Ethan had still been a park ranger at the time, and like most Alaskans, he'd considered the incident a tragic, freak accident. Wolves didn't typically attack people. Everyone knew that. Then, less than thirty days later, he'd watched a bear tear apart a child. Only then had he come to understand the grim difference between *rare* and *never*.

Piper lived alone. Among wolves. Was it possible she would meet the same tragic fate as the schoolteacher from Chignik Lake? Not likely.

But those odds weren't good enough for Ethan. If only this place didn't feel so isolated.

Then again, sometimes it didn't matter, did it? Horrific things could happen, *did* happen, even when help was an arm's length away.

Ethan's phone rang again, and this time he was grateful for the distraction. "Hello."

"Is this Mr. Hale? Ethan Hale?" The woman's voice was unfamiliar, as was the phone number that had popped up on his screen. But he'd recognized the area code. Seattle, Washington.

"Yes, it is," he said.

"This is Anna Plum from *The Seattle Tribune*." Finally. Maybe she'd offer him a job. Right now, so he could walk away from all this wolf business. Unlikely, but it was a nice fantasy. "I received your résumé a while back, and it looks like you're writing some very interesting things up there in Alaska."

"Thank you." She'd actually read the clippings he'd sent. Maybe he really had a shot at this. "What pieces interested you most? I have some updates on the series I did about proposed oil drilling in the Bering Sea."

"That won't be necessary. I was actually referring to your more recent articles, the ones about the wolves."

Just his luck. "The wolf articles. I must admit I'm surprised."

How had she even seen them? The *Yukon Reporter* had an online edition, but its readership was pretty much limited to residents of Alaska.

"Well, you shouldn't be. The AP—Associated Press—has picked them up. You've gone viral, Mr. Hale."

Ethan paused. He simply had no idea what to say. *Viral?* "Is that so?"

"Yes, sir. Congratulations."

He couldn't believe what he was hearing.

"Like I said, we're impressed with your writing, Mr. Hale. We'll be following the rest of your series on the wolf sanctuary, and we'd like you to come out to Seattle to discuss your future. Soon. As soon as possible, in fact."

"I'd like that very much," he said. "But I probably can't get there for another two weeks or so."

"We were aiming for sooner. Is there any way you can make that work?"

Sooner than two weeks? While he was supposed to be cleaning wolf enclosures and writing his column? Doubtful, but his gut told him to get to Seattle as soon as possible. Viral hits didn't exactly last forever, did they? "I'll see what I can do."

"Good. Shoot me an email as soon as you're available." She rattled off her email address, and he jotted it down on a napkin from the Northern Lights Inn coffee bar.

They said goodbye, and Ethan sat staring at his phone. He had ten missed calls and half as many voice mails. What was happening?

You've gone viral.

He should be happy. He knew he should. Somehow this whole scenario didn't feel right, though.

He looked out the windshield toward the first wolf enclosure, where Tundra stood watching him from behind her cluster of aspen trees. Ethan felt the coolness of her copper gaze reaching into the center of his chest like an imperious fist. Why did he get the feeling she was evaluating him somehow? Friend or foe?

I'm not your friend.

He wished the matter were that simple. He wished a lot of things.

He leaned his head against the headrest and squeezed his eyes closed against the memories. What was it about these woods, this snow-covered place of respite, that made him remember so much? It was too much. All of it.

He opened his eyes, and his gaze snagged on something beyond the swirling snow. Something red. His gut clenched.

Was he seeing things?

Maybe it was nothing. Just his mind playing tricks on him again. He climbed out the SUV, and to his horror realized he wasn't imagining things.

Killers.

The word had been scrawled in red paint on the side of Piper's little log cabin office. A big, blood-hued sentiment that could have been plucked straight from Ethan's head, or his newspaper column, and scribed to life.

He felt sick to his stomach all of a sudden. And angry. Furious, even. Which didn't make a whole lot of sense, considering Ethan had used similar terms, if not that exact word, to describe the wolves.

But this was different. Someone had come onto Piper's land and done this. Not to educate, not to inform. But to frighten her.

Ethan's hands began to shake as he stood there staring at it. He felt like hitting something. Something or some*one*.

The trouble was he didn't know who he was more angry at—the idiot who'd defaced Piper's property or himself.

This was his fault. His column had done this. His column that had now gone viral. The so-called feud had gotten out of hand, and now some idiot thought it was okay to come here and terrorize Piper.

Maybe wolves weren't the only dangers lurking in the shadows of her forest.

Ethan's gaze darted to the cluster of hemlock trees to his right and then scanned the horizon. There was no sign of anything else amiss. Nothing. No one. Just the papery bark of the aspen trees, snow soft as feathers and the graceful lope of the watchful wolves.

Fingers numb from the cold, he pulled his cell phone out of the pocket of his parka and dialed Tate Hudson.

He answered on the first ring. "Hudson here."

"Tate, it's Ethan. I'm out at the wolf sanctuary, and we've got a problem." He turned his back on the cabin, but somehow still saw red. He'd probably be seeing red for a long time, at least as long as it took to find whoever had done this.

"A problem?" Tate let out a laugh. "Does the audacious Ms. Quinn have you doing more dirty work today?"

Of course he'd read the article. Everyone from Alaska to the South Pole had read it, apparently. "This is serious. How fast can you get out here?"

Very fast, as it turned out.

Less than twenty minutes later, Tate's police cruiser pulled to a stop alongside Ethan's SUV. By then Ethan had walked the perimeter of Piper's property, searching for signs of more vandalism. He'd come up empty. No more painted messages. And no Piper, either. Which would have given him an immediate ulcer if not for the fact that her car was also absent. She'd probably gone to run an errand or something. Still, he'd feel better when she returned, and he knew she was safely out of harm's way.

Since when is this place safe?

"Any idea when this happened?" Tate snapped a few photos of the graffiti with his cell phone, which Ethan had already done.

"No idea. I got here less than half an hour ago, and I haven't seen Piper. I'm guessing she went into town."

"She couldn't have come outside without noticing this, and we haven't had any calls at the station this morning. Not a one." Tate shook his head and pocketed his phone. "Do you think Piper would have contacted the police if the paint had been here first thing this morning?"

"I'd hope so." But Ethan couldn't say for certain. Piper gave him the impression that she believed she could singlehandedly take on the world, which he found equal parts maddening and captivating.

But she would have been upset if she'd seen this. Extremely upset. Devastated.

Ethan didn't like the thought of a devastated Piper Quinn. Not one bit.

"Maybe she drove into town to report it in person," Tate suggested.

"No." Ethan shook his head. "She wouldn't have left the wolves. Not after something like this."

She would have stayed right here alongside them, all alone, in the middle of nowhere. Unarmed and unprotected. He knew enough about Piper to be certain of that.

"I can dust for prints and take a look around, but I doubt we'll find anything. We usually don't in these circumstances," Tate said. "Unfortunately."

"Should we be worried about this?" *We.* As if he and Piper were a team. A couple. "I mean, do you think she's in danger up here?" Other than the obvious. The wolves.

Tate shook his head. "I doubt it. Aurora's a safe place. You know that, Ethan. Chances are far more likely that this is the work of kids rather than a dangerous criminal. I'd place my bets on someone who's just getting a little too stirred up by what's being printed in the paper these days." He raised his brows at Ethan.

Ethan's jaw clenched. Why did he feel as if he had red on his hands? "All the same, do you think you could keep an eye on her out here? Just in case."

"Sure. I'll make certain we get a patrol car out here regularly, at least until things settle down."

Until you stop attacking one another in the newspaper.

Things had gone too far. It didn't matter if Ethan quit writing the column. It didn't matter if Lou fired him. There was no turning back.

You've gone viral.

It was too late.

Tate crunched through the snow until he stood less than an arm's length from the defaced cabin wall. "With all the snowfall we've been getting this morning, I can't see any obvious footprints. But the paint is definitely fresh. This couldn't have been done more than an hour ago."

So Piper probably hadn't seen it yet. Good.

But she would soon enough. Would it frighten her? Maybe. Would it hurt her? Most definitely. It would stain her heart as surely as it had stained her little log cabin.

One of the wolves howled, a lonely lament that sent a chill up Ethan's spine, and an owl swooped overhead. He forced himself to look at the graffiti again.

Killers.

It left a bad taste in Ethan's mouth. A taste oddly reminiscent of regret.

Chapter Five

Piper was nothing short of giddy as she drove back up the mountain to the wolf sanctuary. She had a plan, a real plan, for getting the rescue wolves back in the community's good graces. At last. Things were beginning to turn around, thanks to Posy.

She'd loved Piper's idea for the recital. The little ballerinas would dance a simplified version of *Little Red Riding Hood*, minus the scary ending, of course. The choreography would chiefly consist of the girls tiptoeing and doing simple ballet steps in red tutus and capes. Liam's youth group could help construct the forest set. And at the end of the dance, after the girls had glided offstage and into the audience, Piper would walk across the stage with Koko on a leash. Just the two of them. It would be the last thing anyone expected. A real wolf.

It was different, just different enough to pack the chairs of Aurora's community center. Hopefully. Posy's dance school and the wolf sanctuary could both use a little boost. A ballet studio and a wildlife rescue center weren't exactly the most obvious allies, but working together made sense.

Even the thought of what Ethan might have to say about the arrangement wasn't enough to put a damper on Piper's excitement. She tried not to think about that as she turned onto the highway that led up the mountain, and waved at the state trooper's car that passed her coming from the opposite direction.

Not thinking about Ethan was difficult, considering his picture stared up at her from the front page of the newspaper she'd tossed onto the passenger seat. She flipped it facedown.

There, that's better.

Why should she worry about Ethan's opinion on the matter, anyway? Other than the fact that he was paid to write about that opinion in the newspaper and all. She shook her head. It didn't matter. Hundreds of people would view one of her wolves at Posy's recital. Once they saw that these rescued animals were actual living, breathing creatures and not crazed monsters, they would understand. Or at least she prayed that they would. She couldn't let Ethan Hale stand in her way. Not this time. These animals had been through enough.

She pulled into the drive of the wolf sanctuary, half expecting to find Ethan waiting for her with his arms crossed and a scowl on his face, ready for battle. Time had gotten away from her at the ballet studio. Now she was late, an infraction for which she'd just chastised him the day before.

But when she climbed out of the van, that wasn't what he was doing at all. She paused and stared, wondering if she was seeing things. Because why on earth would Ethan Hale have taken it upon himself to paint her cabin?

She marched toward him. "What are you doing?"

He tossed her a glance over his shoulder before going back to the task at hand. "Painting."

"I see that." She stood for a moment, wondering what exactly was happening. The gallon of paint that she usually kept stored in the shed was planted beside him in the snow. The brush that she'd just bought a week ago at Aurora's one and only hardware store was in Ethan's manly grasp. The damp cabin wall glistened in the misty morning sunlight. "But why? And how? Where did you find all of this stuff?"

"In the shed." He pointed the paintbrush at her. "Which you need to keep locked from now on, by the way. Anyone off the street could have opened the door and walked right inside. It's a nice heated shed, and you don't even keep it secure. They sell padlocks down at the hardware store, you know."

He was angry. As usual. Although why he cared so much about the fate of her gallon of Olive Branch Green latex paint was a mystery she couldn't begin to fathom.

"Duly noted," she said, waiting for further explanation. Or even a hint as to what was going on.

Wordlessly, Ethan kept moving the brush in long, even strokes. Up, down, swish, swish.

Finally, Piper couldn't tolerate his silence another second. "Ethan, stop."

He gave the area in the middle another dab, stuck the paintbrush handle-side down into the snow and bent to snap the lid back on the gallon of paint. For a man who had so much to say in the newspaper, he was awfully quiet all of a sudden.

"You know the youth group just painted the cottage less than two weeks ago, right? I mean, not that I'm complaining or anything. It just seems like a strange chore to have chosen in my absence. I know I'm late this morning, and—" she had to pray for strength to force out her next words "—I'm sorry."

There. She'd apologized. To Ethan, of all people.

He pounded the lid securely onto the can of paint and stood to meet her gaze. There was something different about the way he looked at her. She felt as light and delicate as a snowflake all of sudden. "It's not a problem. In fact, I'm glad you were away this morning."

Of course he was. Just as she'd been happy to avoid him. Then why did his words sting the way they did? "I see."

"That's not what I meant." Ethan jammed a hand through his hair. He had a dab of green paint near the corner of his mouth, which drew her attention slam-bang to his lips. She wondered suddenly what it might be like to kiss those lips, to kiss Ethan Hale. Her nemesis.

Revolting. *Obviously.* She couldn't think of anything that should disgust her more than kissing Ethan. Nevertheless, her gaze remained stubbornly fixed on his mouth.

"Piper? Did you hear me?" The corners of that mouth, still the focus of her unruly attention, tipped downward in a frown.

She cleared her throat. "Yes, I did. Sorry, you have some paint. Right, um, there."

Without realizing what she was doing until it had become too late, she reached out and touched his face. His cheek was cold beneath her fingertips. Cold and wind-kissed. He didn't flinch or shy away, as she might have done had their roles been reversed, but instead just watched and let her touch him, as if it was the most natural thing in the world. As if her fingertips should alight on that place right next to his mouth and hover so perilously close to his lips.

She forgot to breathe. She forgot everything for a moment, everything but the hard planes of Ethan's chiseled face and the haunted look in his eyes behind the lacy veil of snow that fell between them.

Have you lost your mind? What are you doing? She erased the smudge of paint with the pad of her thumb and pulled her hand away.

"All gone," she managed to whisper.

Why was her hand shaking? And why, oh, why had she gone breathless all of a sudden? It didn't make any sense. None of this did—Ethan painting her cabin, her sudden fascination with his contemptible mouth and, least of all, the unexpected intimacy of the moment.

She shoved her hands in her pockets and prayed for the world to turn right-side-up again. Or alternatively, for him to say something that would remind her why she disliked him so very much.

"Thanks." There was a softness in his gray eyes that she'd never seen before, a softness she could fall into like a feather bed.

She swallowed. What was wrong with her? Feather beds weren't all they were cracked up to be. Everyone knew that. Feather beds were lumpy. And they made people sneeze.

"Listen." Ethan sighed. "When I said I was glad you weren't around earlier, it was because there's been some trouble here."

"Trouble?" she echoed, thoughts of feather beds and floating snowflakes replaced with panic. Heart racing, she spun around and headed for the enclosures. "The wolves. Is everyone okay?"

Ethan tugged on the hood of her parka and reeled her back toward him. "Your precious wolves are perfectly fine."

"Oh." She straightened and took a step away from him, out of reach. "Don't frighten me like that."

It didn't escape her notice when he neglected to apologize. "The cabin was defaced."

She glanced at the damp wall. "Defaced? How?"

"Graffiti. Red spray paint."

Graffiti? In small-town Alaska? Vandalism was the last

thing she should have worried about in a place like this. "Do you know if that happens here often?"

Ethan shrugged and busied himself with washing the paintbrush in a bucket of water. "Tate Hudson thinks it was some bored kids."

That didn't really answer her question, did it? "Tate Hudson? The state trooper? You called the police?"

"It seemed like a good idea, and Tate's a friend." He glanced up from his chore, but didn't quite meet her gaze. "I asked him to stop by and check on things out here regularly. So try not to worry."

Piper wrapped her arms around her middle, hugging herself, and remembered passing the police cruiser on her way up the mountain. Someone had come onto her property and sprayed the cabin with graffiti, the police had been called, and she'd missed the entire thing. Unbelievable.

She felt oddly vulnerable, which was a feeling Piper despised. Her entire existence was pretty much crafted around avoiding it. Feeling weak in any capacity was far too reminiscent of her turbulent childhood. There was a limit to how much vulnerability one person could take, and she'd reached her limit by her eighteenth birthday. Finding out about Stephen's lies had been the icing on the cake.

"Should I? Worry, I mean?" She was forced to speak to Ethan's back, since he was still cleaning up his mess instead of looking at her. Which was fine, really.

The only thing worse than feeling vulnerable would have been to feel vulnerable in front of Ethan Hale.

Tell her.

Ethan hadn't intended on erasing the evidence of all that had transpired at the wolf sanctuary in Piper's absence. He really hadn't. But when he'd accompanied Tate on a final search of the property, he'd spotted the painting supplies in the shed. And seeing them there had seemed like a sign.

A sign. What an odd thing to consider.

Ethan wasn't even sure he believed in signs. Or prayers. Or the God he'd once trusted with all his heart. Not anymore. It had been a long time since anything remotely resembling faith had stirred in his soul. Or anything at all, really.

He'd been numb for the better part of the past five years. He preferred it that way. He'd felt enough for one lifetime already. Too much. Even when his wife had left, he hadn't fallen into despair. He hadn't even tried to persuade her to stay. At the time he'd thought her leaving had seemed only natural. Susan had been looking for a way out of Alaska since the moment they'd set foot there. She'd actually thought his independence was a passing phase and that he'd be working for his father before their first anniversary. That they'd live in an ivory tower somewhere in Manhattan—or even worse, the family hotel—and attend black-tie galas every night of the week.

It had been almost a relief when the divorce papers came. Without Susan there, he didn't have to act as if his life hadn't been torn apart along with that little girl. He didn't have to pretend that he was okay. Because he wasn't. He wouldn't be okay ever again.

Alone, he'd disappeared into the void. Unmoved. Unfeeling. Unbelieving.

Then this morning he'd seen that can of paint in Piper's shed, and he'd almost believed something other than mere chance had put it in his path. Maybe he did believe. Either way, he couldn't bring himself to ignore it.

Still, he knew he had to tell her what the graffiti had said. He had no right to keep it from her.

Killers.

He took too long cleaning the paintbrush while she stood over him, watching, waiting. Too long to brush the snow off the lid of the paint can. When he finally ran out of tasks to prolong the inevitable, he stood and faced her, fully intending to do the right thing.

But the Piper he found looking back at him wasn't one he recognized. The Piper he'd come to know in the past few days was fearless, as much wolf as woman. The Piper standing in front of him here, now, didn't look quite so bold. With her arms wrapped around herself, her fingertips peeking out from behind her fuzzy fingerless gloves, she had a suddenly gentle quality that made Ethan's chest ache.

Tell her.

She blinked up at him through the softly falling snow—snow that felt like a prologue to something bigger. The promise of a coming storm. Looking into her eyes, he saw a world of untold stories, stories he wanted to hear her spin in a cozy cottage, with a fire in the hearth while snow beat against the windows.

He inhaled a ragged breath and told himself these sudden feelings didn't mean anything. He only wanted to protect her, to shield her from hurt and harm. Susan had called it his "superhero complex." After the bear attack, he'd become obsessed. Or so she'd said. Always looking for someone to save, as if that could make amends for the one girl he hadn't.

His ex-wife couldn't have been more wrong. Ethan knew with painful clarity that he was no hero. He couldn't save the girl. He couldn't even save himself. Just as he couldn't be the one to save Piper Quinn.

Tell her. She deserves to know what was written on her cabin.

He opened his mouth, fully intent on confessing the last bit of information he'd withheld. But then he saw the slightest quiver in Piper's lower lip. It was the tiniest of tremors, yet somehow it sent shock waves through Ethan's soul. And he did the one thing he'd sworn to himself he would *not* do, despite the fact that it was all he could seem to think about since the moment she'd so gingerly touched his face. He wrapped his arms around her and pulled her close.

He was unprepared for the way she felt in his arms. It was like holding the most beautiful of wild things. The brightest of butterflies. A bird of paradise. She was exquisite lightness and delicacy, and beneath her tenderness and her vulnerability beat the intensity of a hummingbird heart.

Piper was no ordinary woman. And this was no ordinary embrace. Something about this was different. This wasn't the product of a superhero complex. This was something else. Something warm and soft. Something that made Ethan's heartbeat pulse loudly in his ears. Something that made him feel.

For the first time in so many years, the numbness that had settled over him seemed to be melting away. He felt himself drowning in the scents of pine and peppermint. He felt the icicle bite of the wind in his hair. He felt the gentle kiss of wonderland snowflakes. He actually felt something.

Something for the woman in his arms.

No.

No, no, no.

He wasn't ready. He wasn't ready to feel again, certainly not if those feelings had anything to do with a woman who made her home among wolves. And yet when she stiffened in his embrace, a surge of disappointment shot like an arrow to the center of his once-frozen heart.

He released her and took a backward step. His arms felt strangely useless all of a sudden. Empty.

Tell her. Do it now.

He jammed his hands in his pockets and cleared his throat. "Don't worry. Tate's going to keep an eye on things for you."

"Right." She nodded, but her smile looked forced, her stare vacant. Shell-shocked. "And you'll be around."

"For a while, anyway." Twelve more days. Surely he could go that long without making the mistake of touching her again.

"Awhile. Sure, that's what I meant." She swallowed, looking wounded. Which Ethan supposed was only natural, considering she'd been the victim of a crime. Although she still didn't even know to what extent, since he couldn't bring himself to tell her what the graffiti had said. "I should probably check on the wolves. Sometimes they get spooked when strangers come around, especially when I'm gone."

"You do that." He gestured toward the bucket and can of paint. "I'll finish cleaning up here, and then I'm heading to town."

"To town? What for?"

Distance. Space. A little breathing room to clear my messed-up head.

"To pick up a lock for your shed." He walked past her, painting supplies in tow, before he said something else. Something he shouldn't.

All the while forgetting the words that he should have said most of all.

Chapter Six

To: Anna Plum aplum@theseattletribune.com
From: Ethan Hale ehale@alaskamail.com
Subject: Thank you

Dear Ms. Plum,
Thank you for your call today. I'd appreciate the opportunity to meet you and learn more about the position available at *The Seattle Tribune*. With my experience and background, I believe I could be an asset to your paper. I've attached links to a few of my recent articles on hydropower in the Arctic and the dangers of tsunamis on the Kenai Peninsula.

As we discussed, I'm on assignment at the moment. However, I look forward to making a trip to Seattle as soon as possible.

Thank you again for your time and interest in my work.
Best regards,
Ethan Hale

To: Ethan Hale ehale@alaskamail.com
From: Anna Plum aplum@theseattletribune.com
Subject: RE: Thank you

Hello Ethan,

It was great connecting with you. We at *The Seattle Tribune* are following your wolf diary with avid interest. Please contact me as soon as you have an opening in your schedule.

I look forward to hearing from you at your earliest possible convenience.

Sincerely,

Anna Plum

Editor in Chief

The Seattle Tribune

"What do you think?" Posy held up a tutu that looked too small to fit a wolf cub, much less an actual person.

Piper stared at it, wondering just how miniscule a four-year-old could possibly be. "I think that's the smallest tutu I've ever seen."

"Nope." Posy shook her head. "They definitely come much smaller."

Anya Parker, a friend of Posy's who'd been recruited for the dance school's costume committee, looked up from her needle and thread. "One thing's for sure. It's definitely the reddest."

"Good." Posy grinned. "The theme is *Little Red Riding Hood*, after all."

"And that's large enough to fit a real child?" Piper peered through an opening the size of a nonexistent waist.

"For a four-year-old? Certainly." Kirimi, Anya's mother, gave a reassuring nod. "Little girls are more delicate than you think they are. They're just itty-bitty things."

Piper's throat grew tight.

Little girls are more delicate than you think they are.

She knew exactly how delicate little girls could be. Once upon a time, she'd been one of those delicate girls.

But why was she thinking about that here and now? The church thrift shop was no place for revisiting her mess of a childhood. Until this evening, Piper had never even set foot in the building.

The thrift store was run by Kirimi, Anya's mom. Kirimi was also apparently some kind of sewing genius and had agreed to spearhead the costume efforts for Posy's recital. So they'd all met in the thrift store after hours— Piper, Posy, Kirimi and Anya. The gathering had been a little overwhelming at first. Piper was still growing accustomed to having one close girlfriend, and now suddenly she belonged to a whole group. But their warm welcome soon put her at ease. Aurora was beginning to feel like home.

Piper's heart gave a little squeeze. She'd been so emotional the past few days. She'd feel perfectly fine one minute and then, with no small degree of horror, she'd find herself on the verge of tears the next. It wasn't like her. Not at all. And as much as she wanted to blame her atypical mood swings on the fact that someone had come onto her property and vandalized the cabin, she knew that wasn't the root cause of her weepiness.

No, it wasn't the graffiti. It was Ethan. Ethan, and the way he'd gathered her in his arms and held her while the snow fell around them as if they belonged in a woodland fairy tale.

Even now, three days later, Piper could hardly allow herself to think about it without her face growing hot. She hadn't seen it coming. His actions had caught her completely off guard. And then she'd been so moved by the tenderness of the moment that she'd gone completely stiff in his arms. She'd been unable to move, unable to so much as breathe.

She was fairly certain that Ethan regretted it. He'd given her a wide berth the past few days, speaking to her as seldom as possible. She'd done the same. At least that was her intention. Somehow, her gaze lingered on him a bit too long when he came into view. Once or twice he'd even caught her openly staring.

Her world had gone completely upside down from something as simple as a hug.

She shouldn't feel this way. Ethan might be the man currently painting her cabin and chopping her firewood, but he was doing so under duress. Nothing between them had changed. Nine days from now, they'd say their good-byes and never see one another again.

She should have simply accepted his embrace with a casual pat on the back. But that hadn't been what she'd wanted to do at all. The truth of the matter was that she'd wanted to bury her face in the solid warmth of his chest, to gather the soft folds of his flannel shirt in her fists and hold on for dear life. She'd wanted that very much. The ferocity with which she'd wanted his arms around her had stunned her almost as much as it had frightened her.

She'd gone still out of fear. She needed safety. Security. Those were the very things she'd craved her entire life, even more so after Stephen's betrayal.

Ethan Hale was anything but safe.

Piper jammed her sewing needle into her thumb. *Ouch.* Great. Now she was so distracted by thoughts of Ethan that she was poking holes in herself. Who got so wound up over a simple embrace? She did, apparently.

It was ridiculous. Pathetic, even.

She did her best to ignore the throbbing in her thumb and forced a smile when two more helpers bustled inside the thrift shop.

"Zoey! Clementine! You made it." Posy rose to greet them both with hugs, which they returned with graceful sincerity. Because normal people knew how to hug.

"Sorry we're late," one of the newcomers said. "We stopped by Caleb White's house on the way to drop off some chicken soup. The poor kid has been sick all week."

The mention of Caleb's name was enough to tear Piper away from her thoughts. "How's Caleb doing? He works for me part-time. I know he hasn't been feeling well, and I've been worried about him."

She should've probably been the one delivering chicken soup to the boy, but she'd been a little busy trying to keep things under control at the sanctuary, not to mention the constant effort it took to stop herself from strangling Ethan.

The woman extended her hand. "You must be Piper. I'm Clementine. Caleb is doing a little better, but he hasn't gone back to school yet. Apparently, he's got a really bad case of the stomach flu. Somehow the rest of his family has managed to avoid catching it."

Piper put down her tutu-in-progress and shook hands with her. "That's good, at least. It's nice to meet you."

Clementine's friend tilted her head. "You're Piper Quinn? From the wolf sanctuary?"

A nervous flutter passed through Piper. The town seemed to be dividing itself into two camps—for or against the sanctuary. She wished she knew which side Clementine's friend was on. "Yes, I am."

"I'm Zoey." She smiled. "We're neighbors. My husband, Alec, and I live on the reindeer farm."

Chalk one up for *against*. Probably, anyway. "My wolves aren't trying to eat your reindeer. I promise."

Zoey let out a laugh. "Don't worry. I don't believe everything I read in the paper. Besides, I have a soft spot for animals. All of them."

An animal lover. Perfect. Piper decided right then and

there that she liked Zoey. Very much. "I can't tell you how much I wish that Ethan felt the same way."

Zoey and Clementine exchanged a glance.

"Ethan Hale," Piper said by way of explanation. "He's the reporter doing the series of stories about my wildlife center. He wrote the rather scathing op-ed piece last week."

"Oh, we know who he is." Clementine nodded. "The whole town knows who he is."

The newspaper was still selling like crazy, even though Ethan's rhetoric had toned down a bit since the vandalism. Piper wasn't sure if the change was intentional or not, but his recent diary entries had been informational pieces that described the daily routine at the sanctuary—what the wolves ate and when, how many hours a day they slept. His articles from the past few days hadn't gained her any new enemies, but the wolves weren't exactly making new friends, either. She'd had a grand total of zero visitors in the past two days. None.

"The things he's writing have surprised me," Zoey said. "I'd expect Ethan to have an appreciation for wildlife, given his work experience."

"Does he write about animals often?" Piper asked. Maybe she should have looked up his past articles. A little preparation would have been helpful. *Too late.*

Zoey shook her head. "I don't mean his job with the *Yukon Reporter*. I'm talking about before…when he lived in Denali."

Posy looked up from the puff of red tulle in her lap. "Ethan lived in Denali?"

"Yes, back when Alec lived there. They knew each other." Zoey glanced at Piper. "My husband lived in Denali for a while and worked at the national park."

"I see. Did Ethan write about what went on with the animals at the park?" Piper couldn't help asking. She couldn't imagine Ethan reporting on a national wildlife preserve.

Zoey shook her head. "No, he didn't write about them. He worked with them. He was a park ranger."

Everyone in the room stopped sewing and stared at Zoey. Apparently, Piper wasn't the only one surprised by this bit of information.

Although to say she was surprised would have been a massive understatement. Beyond massive. It was incomprehensible.

"Ethan is a former park ranger?" Anya blinked. "Wow. I never would have guessed."

"Did you know about this, Piper?" Posy asked.

"Um, no. I had no idea." She couldn't wrap her head around it. Ethan Hale. Mr. Wolf Hater. A park ranger? Never had anything made less sense. "Are you sure we're talking about the same Ethan?"

"The one and only. Alec even has a photo of the two of them together. Ethan still worked at the park when Alec left Denali and moved here." Zoey shrugged, as though she hadn't just dropped a gigantic bomb in the middle of the conversation. "So who's going to show Clementine and me what exactly we're doing?"

"Here, it's very simple." Kirimi launched into a tutorial on tutu construction.

Meanwhile, Piper was still reeling. Ethan had been a park ranger. In Denali, of all places.

The wolf population in Denali National Park had been systematically declining for years. There were presently half as many wolves in Denali as there had been just nine years ago. Park rangers were concerned.

At least *some* of them were. Piper had difficulty believing that Ethan had lost any sleep over the reduction in wolf numbers. Anywhere. Even Denali, one of the most beautiful places on earth. Where he'd apparently lived and worked every day, in the shadow of snowcapped Mount McKinley and on the cool blue mirror of Ruth Glacier. It was inconceivable.

Or was it?

She'd spied glimpses of something beneath Ethan's restrained exterior. Something primal and wild. It moved behind his eyes with the natural grace of an alpha. When the wind blew just right, or when snow caught in the stubble that lined his jaw.

When he'd held her.

"So how are things going out at the sanctuary, Piper?" Posy reached across her for a spool of crimson thread.

"Hmm?" Piper blinked.

How long had she been oblivious to the conversation going on around her? Two minutes? Five?

No wonder she'd never had many friends. She was living in another world. A world of memories and wolves and the smell of winter pinecones on Ethan's jacket. It hadn't made sense before, the way nature seemed to cling to him. In some small way, it did now.

But really. She needed to stop thinking about Ethan. And the embrace. She was certain the incident had meant nothing to him. He'd simply been comforting her, as anyone would have done. He'd probably forgotten all about it by now, and here she was, still dwelling on it. Three days later.

So he'd been a park ranger? If it was true—and she still had serious doubts about the notion—it didn't change anything. Clearly. He hated the wolves and, therefore, everything she believed in.

Posy's gaze met hers. And held. "I asked how things were going out at the sanctuary."

"Oh, of course. Thanks for asking." Piper swallowed.

How were things? Surreal. Confusing. Altogether overwhelming. "Fine. Perfectly fine. We haven't had very many visitors. Those that do come seem more interested in the feud between Ethan and me than the wolves. But you know, fine." She breathed out a sigh. "Absolutely fine."

Posy bit back a smile. "So things are fine."

"Yep, totally fine," Piper said. When she looked up from the bundle of red fluff in her lap, she found all four women watching her with undeniable amusement. "What?"

"Nothing." The grin on Zoey's face widened, and she exchanged a knowing glance with Anya.

Then Anya chimed in. "Except that you just told us how *fine* you are no less than four times in the span of a minute."

"I did?" Piper swallowed. Her thumb throbbed from jabbing it with her needle. Yet again. She wished someone would just jam a wad of tulle down her throat so she wouldn't have to say anything for the rest of the night.

Posy shrugged. "I'm afraid so."

"Well, I am." Piper focused intensely on her half-constructed tutu. "Fine, that is."

Clementine nodded. "Clearly."

"Good, because we were a little worried when we heard about the graffiti incident," Posy said.

The graffiti. Of course. One of the many very real, very important things Piper *should* be thinking about.

"I still can't believe someone in Aurora would do such a thing." Kirimi shook her head. "So sad."

Clementine frowned. "I hope you haven't had any more trouble up there."

"We haven't." Piper assured herself that by *we* she meant her and the wolves. Not her and Ethan. "The police have been really good about keeping an eye on things, but so far, so good."

"Have they figured out who did it?" Posy asked.

"Unfortunately, no." Piper shook her head. "The police seem to think it was the work of bored kids."

At least that's what Ethan had told her. She hadn't actually talked to the state trooper about the incident herself. She supposed she should. And she would, when she found the time.

Her to-do list was getting perilously long.

Chapter Seven

Ethan woke with a start and banged his head on something. Hard.

He rubbed his rapidly forming goose egg and tried to shake off the disorientation of being jolted out of his slumber. But by what? And come to think of it, where was he? The crick in his neck and the subarctic chill in the air told him he most definitely was not in his bed. Or the plush king-size bed at the Northern Lights Inn. Or any bed, anywhere.

He opened his eyes, looked around and realized he'd fallen asleep in his car. Again. This was becoming something of a nightly occurrence. What hadn't become part of his routine, however, was seeing Piper's lovely, yet confused, face peering at him through his driver's side window.

Oh, no.

She waved, and Ethan was struck with the nonsensical thought that waking up to the sight of her glacier-blue eyes was rather nice. Too nice.

Then the forlorn melody of a wolf's howl pierced the darkness, and he came to his senses.

He hadn't planned on sleeping at the wolf sanctuary.

He'd just wanted to keep an eye on things to make sure whoever had defaced the cabin wasn't coming back. Tate had kept his promise and was stopping by regularly, but the police couldn't be there twenty-four hours a day.

The night after the graffiti had been found, Ethan had had trouble sleeping. Common sense had told him it was because his head had been resting on a hotel pillow, and he'd made a vow a long time ago to avoid hotels as much as possible. But though he'd hated to admit it, he'd known the reason for his restlessness ran deeper.

He still felt responsible, at least partly, for what had happened. So it had seemed reasonable enough to get in his car and head up the mountain. It had been an attempt to put his mind at ease. To make him stop worrying about Piper up there all alone. It wasn't supposed to become a nightly thing.

Somehow, it had.

He sat up and rolled down his car window, since Piper didn't appear to be going anywhere. "Good evening."

"Good evening?" She narrowed her gaze at him. "It's ten o'clock."

"So it is." Ethan glanced at his watch. It was seven after ten, actually, which meant that Tate would be making another drive-by in approximately eight more minutes.

Ethan would know. He'd witnessed every late-night stop, minus the instances when he'd fallen asleep. The Gold Rush blend coffee from the Northern Lights Inn was good stuff, but caffeine could do only so much. The fact that he couldn't get a wink of sleep in his bed, but seemed to have no trouble falling asleep out here, wasn't something he cared to examine.

"So what exactly are you doing here this time of night? You've been off the clock for hours." Piper's gaze swept the inside of his SUV and lingered on the down sleeping bag spread across his lap. "Oh, no. I think I know what's going on here."

Ethan sighed.

Now she'd no doubt demand to know why he was keeping an eye on her, and he'd be forced to tell her the truth. The rest of it, anyway. He'd have to tell her that the graffiti on her cabin had been a little more serious than he'd let on. Either that, or let her think he was some kind of stalker.

"Ethan." She bit her lip. Given her fearless streak, she seemed far less irritated than he thought she would be. "Why didn't you tell me? I know we're not exactly the best of friends. Actually, you're sort of my enemy…"

Her enemy. So he was either an enemy or a stalker. Neither option was all that flattering.

"…but I could have helped if I'd known." She reached through the open window and gave his arm a squeeze.

He didn't have a clue where this conversation was going, but the simple tenderness of her mittened hand on his arm brought about a sudden tightness in his chest. He cleared his throat. "If you'd known what?"

"That you don't have anyplace to stay." Her hand tightened around his arm in a gesture meant to comfort, to sympathize.

Only then did Ethan understand what was happening. "You think I'm *homeless*?"

"It's nothing to be ashamed of." For once she was looking at him with the same kind of compassion she normally reserved for her wolves. Because she thought he was some helpless creature in need of rescue.

As such, it rubbed him entirely the wrong way. "You can't be serious. Why in the world would you think I'm homeless?"

If Ethan hadn't been so annoyed at the moment, he would have probably pointed out that the northern lights had begun to make a subtle appearance in the sky behind her. He might have told her how their shimmering pink glow looked almost like stars falling into the gold waves of her windswept hair.

She crossed her arms, and he forced himself to focus on her patronizing gaze. "For starters, you're sleeping in your car."

Point taken.

Still. Homeless? He had a home. Counting his room at the Northern Lights Inn, he had two homes at the moment.

Yet here you are, sleeping in your car. At a wolf sanctuary, no less.

"I am not, nor have I ever been, homeless." What would his father say if he knew that his only son, heir to the Pinnacle Hotel fortune, had just been mistaken for a transient person? Ethan let out a little laugh. He couldn't help himself. "Quite the opposite, actually."

Piper lifted a brow. "What does that mean, exactly?"

The lights in the sky behind her deepened to violet, casting her in an ethereal glow that softened Ethan's indignation, no matter how hard he tried to keep a grasp on it.

"It means that I grew up in a home that had six hundred and sixty-eight rooms, not including ballrooms and the like," he said quietly.

She rolled her eyes. "Right."

"I'm not joking. Six hundred and sixty-eight rooms. Thirty-one floors." Over one thousand crystal chandeliers. He left out that particular detail. Why he was telling her any of this at all was a mystery.

He blamed it on his semiconscious state. Or possibly the auroras.

The notion that the aurora borealis, or the northern lights, had any significant meaning was antiquated. They were a natural scientific phenomenon. Nothing more. But the beauty of the lights was undeniably haunting, and since the beginning of time, myths and legends had been created to explain their sudden appearances. He'd even heard them called *revontulet*, which was Finnish for *fox fire*. In Finland, the lights were so named for a fox sweeping its tail across the snow, spraying it up into the sky.

Strange. Ethan hadn't thought about the fanciful fox story in a long while. And he couldn't remember the last time he'd seen an aurora, although he could recall with perfect clarity the first night he'd witnessed one.

He'd been awake for more than twenty-four hours straight, pulling an all-nighter at the park after illegal trapping activity had been uncovered in the area. They'd lost one coyote, and another had been severely injured. Their pack had been reluctant to leave. They'd kept circling Ethan as he'd carried the hurt animal along the banks of the Last Fork River, yelping and howling. A coyote's cry was so distinctive that once you heard it, it lived in your memory until the day you died. That night, in particular, their eerie melody seemed to brand itself on Ethan's soul. Then a wisp of amber had appeared above him, so faint that he'd thought he was imagining things. It faded in and out, growing larger and more luminous until the entire horizon glittered like a canary diamond.

Cradling that coyote in his arms, hands and face numb from the cold, Ethan had looked at the shimmering sky and realized he was the happiest he'd ever been. He was doing something he loved, something meaningful, and had never felt so much a part of nature. So close to God. Words he'd read in Sunday school as a child had come flooding back, like a gift from an unseen hand.

And I looked and, behold, a whirlwind came out of the north, a great cloud, and a fire enfolding itself, and

*a brightness was about it, and out of the midst thereof as
the color of amber, out of the midst of the sky.*

Those memories belonged to a different man. A man
Ethan no longer knew. But right here, right now, with a
halo of amethyst light surrounding Piper's exquisite, delicate features, that man didn't feel so far away.

Ethan's chest grew tight. He tore his gaze from her and
focused instead on the frayed sleeping bag in his lap.

"You grew up in a home with *seven hundred* rooms?"
she said, teeth chattering from the cold. "Who *are* you?"

Good question.

"Do you want to get in, and I'll explain?" He leaned
over and pushed open the passenger side door.

"Okay."

He expected her to hesitate, but she didn't. She bounded
around the front of the car, her breath dancing in the wind,
hair streaming behind her. Pink ribbons in the light of the
violet Alaskan sky.

She slid onto the bench seat beside him in a rush of
winter air, enveloping him in the scent of snow and evergreens. "So tell me about your family's castle. Did it have a
turret and a moat? Don't tell me…you had a fire-breathing
dragon as a pet, too."

"Yes. A rescue dragon, actually. Poor thing grew up in
the bathtub of a boy's dorm room."

"That story sounds vaguely familiar." She pulled off
her red mittens and gave him a playful smack with them.
"I'm impressed."

"By the castle? Don't be."

"No, silly. By the fact that you actually made a joke."
Her smile seemed lit from within, and Ethan realized it
wasn't the northern lights that were casting a glow over
the moment. It was her.

What was he doing? He should be asleep in bed right

now. He definitely shouldn't be here, telling her about his childhood. "It was a hotel, not a castle. The Pinnacle in Manhattan. My family—my father, rather—owns it."

"Oh. Wow." She looked at him as if he'd just sprouted wings. "So you're rich."

"No. My father is rich. Big difference." It was a massive difference. Big enough to drive a wedge between him and Susan long before his troubles after the bear attack had permanently changed things. "Besides, growing up in a luxury hotel isn't all it's cracked up to be. Trust me."

"You mean you'd rather be wrapped up in a sleeping bag in the front seat of a car in subzero temperatures?" she asked, her voice going almost unbearably soft.

It was moments like this, when he caught a glimpse of her softer side, that his own walls began to fall. Being gentle and open didn't come easy to her. Ethan knew as much. He understood better than anyone the need to hide behind a fearless exterior.

His chest grew uncomfortably tight. "Something like that, yes."

"You are full of surprises, Ethan Hale." She fixed her gaze on his, and it was as if she were seeing him for the first time. The real him.

And it was too much. Too much exposure, too much light, like walking into the sunlight after years spent in darkness. A beautiful, blinding delirium.

Then she asked him a question, and the light became sickeningly bright. "Why haven't you told me that you came to Alaska to be a park ranger?"

Ethan grew very still. He couldn't have heard her right. "Ethan?"

He cleared his throat. "How did you find out?"

"I was at the church thrift store tonight helping out with

a…um, project, and Zoey Wynn was there. She said that you worked at Denali National Park with her husband."

Only a handful of people in town knew about his past. Of course Piper would become friendly with one of them. Just his luck. "Ah. I see."

"You act like you despise everything to do with the wilderness. You let me go on and on about the National Nature Conservatory. You've even seen me struggling with all the grant paperwork when you could have helped. I barely got the application in on time. Why didn't you say something?"

"Because it's not something I talk about." Why was he still sitting here having this conversation? He'd already exposed more of himself than he had to anyone in a long time. A *very* long time. He wasn't ready to go down this road. Not with her. Not with anyone.

"I don't understand, Ethan. Talk to me. Help me understand." She rested her hand on his arm again, this time without her mitten. Skin on skin. The butterfly delicacy in her touch told him that she could carry his truths in gentle hands, and Ethan felt something inside him begin to unfold. "Please."

He made the mistake of looking into her eyes, filled with tender invitation. And he couldn't stop the words. He simply couldn't hold them in any longer. "There was a bear."

"A bear?" Her forehead creased in confusion. "In Denali?"

He nodded. "A grizzly. It attacked a camper in the park, and I was there. I saw the whole thing. I tried to help. I tried screaming. I hit the bear. I pulled out fistfuls of its hair. I tried everything. Everything…" His voice had grown hoarse, his throat raw from the rustiness of the things he'd been unable to say for so long.

"Oh, no." Piper's hand fluttered to her heart. "Please, no."

But Ethan could tell that she already knew how the story ended. She just didn't want to believe it.

"It was only the second fatal bear mauling in the park's history. A freak accident. That's what everyone called it." Ethan swallowed. With great difficulty. "But they weren't there. They didn't see what I saw. Things I can never forget, no matter how hard I try."

"So you left Denali?"

"Yes. I couldn't stay there. I tried. I was married at the time, to my high school sweetheart. Things hadn't been going well. Truth be told, they never had, even from the start of the marriage. We were too young, too naive. The mauling was the final straw. She went back to New York, and I ended up here."

He wasn't sure how long they sat in silence after he'd told Piper his story. Two minutes? Ten? Long enough for Ethan to become painfully aware of the feeling blooming between them like a tremulous bud pushing through the snow. Rare and beautiful. But doomed.

"I came here after a breakup, too," she said quietly.

Ethan couldn't have been more surprised. She'd never mentioned a prior relationship. It seemed silly to think that her closest ties had always been with the wolves, but that's what he'd assumed. "You were married?"

"No." She shook her head. "Engaged."

"It didn't work out?"

She let out a little laugh that was laced with far more pain than humor. "I found out he was already married. He had an entire family that I knew nothing about. So no, it didn't work out."

"Piper…"

"Don't feel sorry for me. Please. It was for the best." She nodded. "He lied. Why would I ever want to be with someone who lied to me like that?"

He lied.

Ethan's gut churned, and the word *Killers* flashed in his mind like a warning sign. He still hadn't told her why he was so worried about her and the sanctuary. He needed to explain. He didn't want to be another man who lied to her.

He gazed out the window at the snow. It looked almost like cotton candy beneath the soft lights of the auroras, and he couldn't do it. He couldn't ruin the sweetness of this moment. Not just yet.

"Come inside for a while? Please." There was a tremble in her voice that foretold of the breaking of walls. Of wills. And Ethan knew without a doubt that if he didn't leave at once, he would cradle her lovely face in his hands and kiss her obstinate mouth. "You must be freezing. I've got cocoa. I'll even forgo the marshmallows, since you're not a fan."

How easy it would be to follow her inside her cozy cabin and talk into the wee hours while the auroras swirled overhead. To believe that his presence here had more meaning than just words on a page. To believe that maybe, just maybe, he'd found his way to this place for a reason.

Never had it seemed so easy to believe.

But he couldn't. Not anymore. And certainly not with her, the wolf woman. Here in the close quarters of the car, with snow billowing around them outside the windows, it felt as if they were somehow protected from the real world. Secluded in their own little snow globe. But that wasn't reality. Seattle was waiting. It was time to start over. His new life would be a safe one, in a big, anonymous city. No more bears. No more wolves. No more memories. "I should be getting back."

"To your hotel," she said flatly. Her next words weren't spoken, but heavily implied. *Because you love hotels so much.*

He forced a smile. "Yes, to my hotel."

"I understand."

No, you don't. I don't understand it myself.

She reached for the door handle, then paused. "Ethan, why are you here? You never told me."

"I couldn't sleep, so I thought I'd go for a drive. I just wanted to make sure everything was okay up here." He nodded toward the wall on the cabin where the graffiti had been scrawled.

"But the police are keeping an eye on things, and we've had no more trouble." Her lips parted ever so slightly, and the ache in Ethan's chest became an actual physical pain. "Tell me the real reason. I think there's more to it than the graffiti."

Of course there was more to it than that. More than he could admit even to himself. More than he could articulate, when every thought in his head revolved around kissing her.

Time was running out. He needed to put a stop to this. Now, while he still could. "It's late, and you can stop looking at me like that. I'm not one of your wolves, Piper."

She flinched. His words had hit their mark with the desired effect. "I don't... I mean..."

What was wrong with him? He was a mess. And an idiot. Such an idiot that he kept talking when he should have shut his mouth. "I don't need a champion, Piper. And I don't need saving."

An awful silence fell upon them, a quiet that cut to the bone. She gathered her mittens and coat, pushed the door open and fixed her gaze on him, eyes shining bright. "You sure about that?"

She'd seen right through him. Probably because he'd never told a bigger lie in his life. "Piper, wait—"

But it was too late to apologize. Before he could get another word out, she slammed the car door in his face.

He watched her walk away until the swirling snow hid her from sight. Only then did Ethan lift his gaze to the sky, finding it dark and empty. A silent, limitless void. The auroras…they'd gone, leaving him to wonder if he'd only imagined them all along.

Do not *look back. Don't do it.*

Piper's hands shook as she jammed her key in the front door of the cabin. Her furious exit from Ethan's SUV would have been far more effective if she could have kicked up some snow in her wake, but the walkway was clear. Apparently someone had shoveled it for her. Someone who she felt like strangling at the moment.

Chalk up another good deed for Ethan Hale. He didn't even have the decency to play the part of villain properly so that she could feel good about despising him. It was infuriating.

And humiliating. Because for a moment there, she'd thought something was happening between them. At last she'd thought she'd understood him. He'd shared his life with her, his pain, and she'd never seen a man so conflicted. So beautiful.

She'd thought he was about to kiss her. What's more, she'd *wanted* him to kiss her. Very much. The intensity with which she'd wanted it had been altogether terrifying.

I'm not one of your wolves, Piper. I don't need a champion, and I don't need saving.

How could she have misread things so thoroughly?

Ethan didn't feel anything for her. He didn't want her. *Nobody ever does.*

To top it off, he'd apparently been born with a silver spoon in his mouth. Could they possibly have less in common?

And yet…

He'd turned down his family's millions—maybe even billons—to come to Alaska and work as a park ranger. She hadn't been imagining those hidden glimpses of a man who felt at home in the woods, among the wind, the trees and her beloved wolves. That was the real Ethan. Somewhere, deep down, buried beneath the pain, that man still lived. The bear hadn't killed that man. She knew it hadn't. She also knew she might even be able to love a man like that.

If he would let her.

He didn't want her. Piper shouldn't have been so upset. She and rejection were old friends. She didn't know why Ethan's dismissal bothered her so much. Beyond what he wrote about her in the newspaper, nothing he thought mattered. At least it shouldn't. Yet it did.

Maybe because despite all his insistence to the contrary, she had the distinct feeling that no one needed saving more than Ethan Hale. But he was right. She wasn't the one to save him. The man was full of secrets. And she rescued wolves, not people.

She threw her keys on the kitchen counter and watched his headlights disappear from view through the sheer curtains on the front window. *Good riddance.* He was gone, and suddenly she felt unbearably lonely.

Her throat grew tight, and everything that had gone on in the past year started pressing in on her. Things she'd managed to not think about in the day-to-day business of life—the ring Stephen had given her on her last birthday, the picture that had fallen out of his wallet that same night when he'd reached for his credit card at dinner, the sickening feeling in the pit of her stomach when she'd seen the smiling faces in the photo. A wife. Two small children.

Piper had known without having to ask. Somehow she'd just known. He'd tried to explain, begged her not to leave, promised to leave his family. Maybe. Eventually.

As if that would have made a difference. She could never have anything to do with breaking apart a family. Families were sacred. Holy. Even more so for someone who'd never been a part of one.

She squeezed her eyes closed. She didn't want to think about that night any more than she wanted to think about how happy she'd been to find Ethan's car in her driveway when she'd come home from the tutu-making party. How could she have been so stupid? Again.

She grabbed a winter hat, wound her hair up in a makeshift bun and tucked it inside. Then she pulled her mittens on, zipped her parka all the way closed and walked back outdoors. The moon hung low, swollen and as creamy white as a pearl. She remembered that a February full moon was sometimes called a snow moon, and she could see why, here in this land of perpetual winter.

She didn't mind the cold. It made her feel more alive, more connected to the world around her. She liked being able to see her breath in the air. She liked the way she could sometimes catch the scent of pine and slow-burning firewood on her clothes, in her hair. As if Alaska were imprinting itself on her, the way wolf cubs imprinted on their mothers.

Imprinting—a lifelong, unbreakable connection to a specific thing—was crucial for wolves. It was what cemented the bond between mother and child. In wolves, it happened when a wolf cub first opened its eyes. The cub saw its mother, and for the rest of its life, looked to her for survival. For comfort. The wolf mother experienced the same phenomenon as she looked into her little cub's eyes. Biology told her that this tiny creature was a part of her. It was her child, to care for and protect. Forever. A wolf's eyes fluttered open and a lifelong bond was formed. Unbreakable.

Piper thought it was possibly the most beautiful thing she'd ever heard. She wished that human biology could be so simple. What if when a mother first looked into her child's eyes, an everlasting, unshakable love was born? What if love, real love, happened with something as simple as a glance? Love at first sight. Between a mother and child. Between a man and a woman.

She wished that was how things worked. She wished it so very much. But people were people, and wolves were wolves.

Eyes glowing in the thick darkness, Koko loped toward the fence to meet her. He paced back and forth as she unlocked the gates to his enclosure. First one, then the other.

"How's my boy, huh? How's my sweet, sweet boy?" she cooed as he rose up on his hind legs in greeting.

This was what she needed. This. The solace of her wolves. Not her long-lost mother. Not Stephen. Not Ethan Hale. The wolves were her family now. They were imprinted on her heart. They were hers. And they were enough.

They had to be.

She buried her fingers in the velvety cold comfort of Koko's fur, let him lick the salty tears from her face and wondered when she'd begun to cry.

Chapter Eight

To: Ethan Hale ehale@alaskamail.com
From: Anna Plum aplum@theseattletribune.com
Subject: Touching base

Hello Ethan,
I'm just touching base with you to see how your schedule looks for the coming week, and if you've managed to find time to pay us a visit.

    My assistant would be happy to arrange transportation on your behalf. I look forward to hearing from you.
Sincerely,
Anna Plum
Editor in Chief
The Seattle Tribune

"The caffeine is on me." Lou plunked a mug down on the coffee bar the next morning and slid it toward Ethan. "Because you look terrible, and I do mean terrible."

"Thanks. I think." Ethan closed the email browser on his phone, scrubbed his hands over his face and pressed the heels of his palms against his closed eyelids. He was sick of this place. Sick of the Northern Lights Inn. Sick of the miserable grizzly bear in the corner. Sick of Alaska. Sick of making a mess of things.

Sick of all of it.

But Lou was still his boss, at least for the time being. Ethan needed this job, so it was probably best to make an attempt to look enthusiastic. Or at the very least, awake. He sat up straighter on his bar stool.

Lou gave him a sideways glance. "Seriously, what does the wolf woman have you doing up there? Running laps around the mountain? Because you look bad."

"I didn't get much sleep last night, that's all. I'm fine." He forced a smile. He wasn't fine. He kept hearing the awful things he'd said to Piper the night before. They went round and round in his head in a continuous loop.

I'm not one of your wolves.

She was kind. She was compassionate. She was real. And he'd taken that extraordinary authenticity of hers and thrown it back in her face.

His head hurt, along with his heart. "Is that what this urgent breakfast meeting is about, Lou? My appearance?"

Ethan's phone had begun ringing at six o'clock. Again. These early-morning calls from his editor were becoming a habit. He'd ignored it the first time. But less than two minutes later, when his phone rang again, he'd managed to rouse himself and take the call. Ethan could think of only a handful of reasons his boss would want to drive to Aurora and talk to him first thing in the morning, and none of those reasons were pleasant. Then again, the last time Lou had demanded to see him like this he'd given Ethan his own column on the front page. So maybe things were better than they seemed.

Lou shook his head. "Things are not good, Ethan. Not good."

So much for optimism.

He slapped the morning edition of the *Yukon Reporter* on the coffee bar and stabbed at Ethan's thumbnail photo with his pointer finger. "Do you mind telling me what this is?"

Ethan flinched. *My face?* "Is there a problem with my column today, Lou?"

"Yes. Absolutely there's a problem." Lou tugged at his tie, and his face reddened a shade or two. Never a good sign. "Read it."

"You want me to read my own column?" Lou's behavior was bordering on ridiculous. Which could only mean he was even angrier than Ethan had realized. But why?

"Yes. Right now, while I wait." Lou pushed the newspaper toward Ethan.

He took it and reread the article he'd turned in just prior to ten o'clock last night, before he'd made his ill-fated trip back to the wolf sanctuary. He'd proofread it for mistakes and typos, but maybe he'd missed something. He hadn't exactly been giving his work his full attention lately.

But the piece read clean. He couldn't figure out what his boss was so upset about. "Help me out here, Lou. I still don't see anything wrong with it."

"There's nothing wrong with what you wrote. There is, however, something very wrong with what you *didn't* write." He snatched the newspaper from Ethan's hands, flipped it to the center page and spread it open on the bar. "A rather glaring omission, don't you think?"

At first Ethan didn't know what he was supposed to be looking at. The page Lou had offered up for inspection was the section reserved for local personal interest news. Bake sales, craft fairs, church picnics. That sort of thing. The editor in chief of the paper didn't even oversee this section. Final copy was approved by a junior editor.

Case in point—the article at the very top centered

around an upcoming dance recital. Ethan scanned the piece, just in case. "Tap, jazz, ballet." Blah blah blah. "The recital will feature a fairy-tale theme, with dancers playing the parts of Cinderella, Snow White, Rapunzel, and even Little Red Riding Hood."

Ethan's gut churned.

Little Red Riding Hood?

He forced himself to keep reading, hating the direction his imagination was headed. Surely this had nothing to do with Piper and her wolves. It just wasn't possible. But there it was, in black-and-white print...

"The grand finale of the recital will include an appearance by a live wolf from the Aurora Wolf and Wildlife Sanctuary. Don't miss this chance to see Aurora's youngest ballerinas and a real wolf, up close and in person!"

Up close. In person. At a *children's* dance recital?

"No." Ethan shook his throbbing head. "This isn't happening."

"Oh, it's happening. In less than two weeks." Lou stared at the page. "Are you telling me that you knew nothing about this?"

"Not a thing."

"Can you explain to me how it is that I've given you prime placement on the front page of my newspaper and gotten you all day, every day access to the wolf sanctuary, and yet you seem to have no idea what's going on there?" An angry vein throbbed in Lou's forehead. Ethan wouldn't have been surprised if his skull exploded.

He might even be able to understand if it had. His boss had every right to be angry. Ethan should have known about this. How had he missed it?

He strained for a memory of any indication, even the slightest hint, that Piper had planned something like this. He knew she was friendly with the ballet teacher, but she hadn't breathed a word about a dance recital, much less the preposterous notion of a wolf in attendance.

He shook his head. "I don't know…" Then he paused. "Wait, she mentioned something last night. Some sort of project that she'd been working on at the church thrift store."

Now that he thought about it, he realized she'd been awfully vague about where she'd been the night before. He could have asked her. He *should* have asked her. But he hadn't.

"It doesn't matter now, does it?" Lou wadded the paper into a ball and pitched it into the trash can on the side of the coffee bar.

Ethan sighed. "Am I fired?"

He almost wished Lou would say yes. This entire ordeal was turning into an even bigger headache than Ethan had anticipated. He'd expected trouble from the wolves. He'd expected trouble grappling with his memories. But he'd never expected the conflicting feelings that Piper drew out of him. Last night he'd have offered up his family fortune to kiss her. And now…

He couldn't have possibly been angrier with her. She'd kept this from him. Intentionally. He knew it as surely as he knew that snow was white.

"I can't fire you. Things are certain to heat up now that this recital is on the horizon. But I need you to get your head on straight. Get some sleep, for crying out loud. And find out what the wolf woman is up to, would you? Don't let her out of your sight. Understood?"

"Yes." Ethan nodded grimly.

Don't let her out of his sight? How was he going to manage that and somehow get to Seattle for an interview?

He'd figure it out. He had no choice. He couldn't keep putting off Anna Plum. She was the editor in chief of a major newspaper. Finally, he might have a chance to move on and leave Alaska behind him. As far as he was concerned, the interview in Seattle couldn't come quickly enough. Surely he could hold out until he managed to get out of Alaska without losing his mind.

Don't let her out of your sight.

Then again, maybe not.

Piper somehow successfully managed to traverse the snowy sidewalks of downtown Aurora all the way from the Northern Lights Inn coffee bar to Posy's ballet school, while at the same time balancing a cardboard tray of coffee cups in each hand. Then she saw Ethan leaning against the white gingerbread trim of the building with his arms crossed and his gray eyes full of thunder, and her concentration slipped.

What was he doing at the ballet school? And so early in the morning?

She wasn't prepared to see him yet. Not after the awkwardness of the night before. She'd planned on putting in an hour or two with the recital committee, working on props, before facing him at the wolf sanctuary. Clear her head. Take her mind off things. Specifically, off him.

But here he was. Glowering. Waiting. For her?

Goodness, she hoped not.

Then he spotted her, pushed off the wall and planted himself in her path. Waiting for her indeed.

Piper tried her best to pretend she didn't see him. She tried so hard that in all her concentration, she lost her footing on an icy patch of pavement. Her hiking boots slid like ice skates until she glided to a stop directly in front of Ethan. The coffee cups, however, kept moving. Before she could stop them, six cups of Gold Rush blend upended themselves, tumbled to the ground and landed with a caffeinated splash on Ethan's impatient feet.

Oh, no.

She stared down at the mess, too shocked to do much else.

Ethan glanced at his boots and frowned. "Am I imagining things, or do you have a vendetta against every pair of footwear I own?"

"I'm sorry." She squatted and dabbed at the mess with a handful of flimsy napkins from the coffee bar. Her efforts were wholly ineffectual, but she kept at it because she'd rather do anything—even wash his feet, biblical-style—than look him in the eye at the moment. "So, so sorry."

Dab, dab, dab.

The napkins began to disintegrate in her hands.

"Piper." His voice was deadly calm. "Stand up."

She obeyed, chastised herself for doing so, then squatted again. He couldn't order her around. He wasn't her boss. It was the other way around, wasn't it?

This is ridiculous. She was making the whole situation more uncomfortable. Who knew such a thing was even possible?

She gave one of his feet a final dab with a wet shred of napkin and then stood. "There."

"All finished?" he asked, looking far too smug for her liking.

"I suppose." She wiggled her nose. He reeked of coffee now. And probably would for all eternity. "Again, sorry. You startled me. I didn't expect to see you here."

He lifted an irate brow. "I'll bet you didn't."

She swallowed and reminded herself that she didn't have a single thing to feel guilty about. She'd done nothing wrong. Except shower his feet in hot coffee, that is. "What are you doing here, Ethan?"

"My job."

"But your job isn't here. It's at the wolf sanctuary. And it doesn't start for…" She reached into her pocket for her cell phone and glanced at the time. "Another hour and twenty minutes."

"Not that job, lovely. My real job. I'm not always a poop scooper for wolves. I'm a professional reporter, remember?"

As if she could forget such an annoying detail. Even more annoying—the way she went all fluttery inside when he called her "lovely," despite the fact that it dripped with sarcasm. "How could I forget?"

"Did you think I wouldn't find out about this?" He pulled a folded sheet of pink paper from the pocket of his parka and whipped it open inches from her face.

Piper didn't need to read it. She'd seen dozens of fliers just like it already. In fact, she'd helped tack them up all over downtown Aurora after the tutu party. "Posy's recital? I had no idea you had such a keen interest in dance."

"Enough." He thrust the flier at her again. "Why didn't you tell me about this?"

She shrugged. "Why would I? You would have only told me what a terrible idea it was."

"Maybe because it *is* a terrible idea," he fumed.

She told herself not to let his criticism get to her, especially in light of the things he'd shared with her last night. But it was awfully difficult to ignore the disapproval in his tone. "Ethan…"

"You're *not* doing this." He waved the flier like a madman.

"Yes I am, Mr. Bossy Pants. You can't stop me." Didn't he see that this was all his doing, anyway? "First, you drive away all my visitors by saying such awful things in the newspaper, then you refuse to help me with grant paperwork and now you're trying to tell me I can't participate in a community event. It's not going to work this time."

"You can participate all you want. Put on a pair of ballet shoes and pirouette across the entire Yukon for all I care." His arm waving kicked into overdrive. He really needed to calm down. People all up and down the sidewalk were beginning to stare. "Your wolves, on the other hand..."

"*Wolf.* Singular. It's Koko, and he wouldn't harm a fly. You should know that by now." Seriously. Where had Ethan been for the past week?

He crossed his arms and glared down at her. "Is this the same Koko who ate the shoes right off my feet?"

He had to bring that up again, didn't he? She lifted her chin and glared right back. "I'm beginning to think you have an unhealthy attachment to your shoes. Who are you, Carrie Bradshaw?"

"Piper." He said it like a warning rather than a name. She almost wished he'd go back to calling her "lovely."

"I don't know why you're so angry," Piper said. "I'm the one who's been wronged. Not you." An awkward silence fell between them. Because she actually did understand now. A little, at least.

All those awful things he'd penned about her wolves? He hadn't written them about Koko or Tundra or Shasta. He'd been writing about the bear. That bear was behind all this.

She sighed. "Ethan, can't you see what's happening? You've made it nearly impossible for the sanctuary to survive."

"And you nearly got me fired this morning, so we're even."

She blinked. "Fired? How?"

He jerked his all-too-handsome head in the direction of the ballet school. "Let's just say that my editor was less than thrilled to discover I knew nothing about your scheme to put a wolf in a tutu."

"Oh. I'm sorry. I didn't mean to get you in trouble. I'm just trying to stay solvent." Which was looking more impossible by the minute. "Lou's not actually going to fire you, is he?"

"Not unless I get scooped again by another reporter. Which will definitely not happen, because I've been ordered to not let you out of my sight." Ethan gave her a tight smile, and she honestly couldn't tell whether he hated the prospect of being stuck to her like glue or kind of liked it.

But he couldn't possibly be fond of the idea. It sounded loathsome on every level.

"Right." She rolled her eyes.

"I'm serious. Where you go, I go."

He had to be joking. She couldn't walk around with Ethan stuck to her side for the remainder of his time at the sanctuary. She simply could *not*. "I believe that's considered stalking."

He shrugged. "Call the police. I've got Tate Hudson's number right here." Ethan offered her his phone.

She had a mind to snatch it and hit him over the head with it. "Fine. Loiter out here all you want. I'm going inside. I've got a committee meeting to attend."

Before Ethan could give voice to the snide comment that Piper was certain he had at the ready, the door to the dance studio opened and Posy poked her head outside.

"Good morning, you two." Her gaze flitted back and forth between them. Piper completely ignored the mess on Ethan's feet, as if having coffee tossed at him were a daily occurrence. Which it should be, as far as she was concerned. "Is everything okay out here?"

"We just had a little coffee accident, that's all." Which Piper had completely absolved herself from, seeing as

Ethan was pretending nothing whatsoever had transpired between them the night before, and had gone back to being his insufferable self. "I'm ready to get to work and help make some papier-mâché trees."

"For goodness' sake, come inside and get out of the cold." Posy held the door open.

Piper bent to pick up all the empty coffee cups and cardboard trays, then stood and gave Ethan a final nod. "It was nice to see you, Ethan." *Not.*

But when she climbed the studio steps, she didn't need to turn around to know that he'd followed right on her heels. His presence behind her was too intense to ignore.

She spun around. "Do not follow me in here, Ethan. Honestly."

"Um, Piper, he's not following you," Posy said, offering Ethan a smile that he returned with saccharine sincerity. Piper somehow managed not to throw up. "Ethan called me this morning and volunteered his services for the recital committee. I said yes, of course. The more, the merrier. Right?"

Seriously?

I've been ordered not to let you out of my sight.

Piper stared at Ethan, aghast.

"The more, the merrier," he echoed, and as soon as Posy turned her back, he shot Piper a triumphant wink. "Right, Piper?"

"Right," she muttered, and did her best to ignore the way his wink skittered through her in a riot of shivers.

Ugh.

Chapter Nine

Piper dropped the coffee mess in the trash and hung her parka on one of the hooks lining the wall in the entryway of the dance studio. Ethan hung his coat on the neighboring hook. No doubt on purpose. Their parkas hung side by side, arms touching, and for some silly reason a lump formed in Piper's throat.

Ridiculous. She swiveled to face Ethan. "I don't know what you think you're going to accomplish. We're not even discussing Koko this morning. We're working on props."

"So you say." He gave her a playful tap on the nose. The fact that his placement on the recital committee had clearly annoyed her seemed to take the edge off his anger.

Piper wondered if it was indeed too late to get him fired. Not that she actually would, tempting as it might be. "We'll see how smug you are once you're elbow-deep in papier-mâché."

He pushed up the sleeves of his sweater, exposing those gorgeous nonwriterly forearms of his. Probably because they were actually *park ranger* forearms. "Bring it on, lovely."

She *really* wished he would stop calling her that. "I can't deal with you right now. I just can't. I'm going to walk to the other side of the room, and it would be *lovely* if you would stay here."

She turned on her heel and headed for Posy's coffee-maker, since she'd dumped her morning caffeine fix, plus everyone else's, on his feet. What a phenomenal waste of good coffee.

As she filled the coffeepot with water, the remaining members of the committee arrived—first Anya and her mother, followed by Clementine, then Zoey. Posy made sure everyone knew Ethan, and he was given an exceptionally warm welcome. Piper assured herself this was because they were nice people, not because anyone was particularly thrilled to see him there. At least she hoped so.

She gave the can of coffee an unnecessarily hard shake before opening it. Her attitude was appalling, and she knew it. Posy really did need the help. The recital was in a little more than a week.

Forgive me, Lord.

Since she'd befriended Posy and Liam and had been stopping by the church pretty regularly, Piper had begun talking to God a little bit. She wasn't sure when she'd started, exactly, but in spite of all that had gone wrong since she'd moved to Alaska, she somehow had the feeling that many things had fallen into place. And all those things were in some way related to the church. Like Caleb and the other kids from the youth group. And becoming involved with Posy's recital. And friends. Actual friends. Piper had begun to wonder if maybe God was looking out for her. Maybe He'd been looking out for her all along.

It was a strange thing to consider, given her childhood. But she had the wolves. Saving them had, in turn, saved her. Maybe the wolves were a gift from Him.

She didn't know. Sometimes she liked to think so, though.

"Thank you for bringing Ethan along this morning," Zoey said, moving beside her and reaching in the cabinet overhead for coffee mugs.

"Don't thank me. I had nothing to do with it."

"I'm quite sure you did." She tore open a packet of sweetener and sprinkled it in one of the cups. "If not for you, he wouldn't be here."

That was technically true, but the actual situation wasn't quite so flattering. "He's stalking me as part of his job. Trust me, he doesn't want anything to do with the recital. He's one hundred percent against Koko and me taking part. He's probably got some sort of sabotage plan up his sleeve."

Zoey rolled her eyes. "Don't take this the wrong way, but you sound a tad paranoid."

"Not paranoid." Piper shook her head. "*Realistic*. Ethan and I are archenemies."

"Like Batman and Catwoman?" Zoey said.

Piper laughed. "Yes, although I'm a bit surprised to hear you use that analogy."

Zoey shrugged. "I dropped off some comic books for Caleb yesterday. He's still stick, but he's on the mend. He can't wait to go back to work at the sanctuary. It's all he talked about. He's been saving Ethan's articles. Every last one."

"He should stick to comic books. They're better reading than Ethan's libelous column." The brew cycle of the coffeemaker finally switched off. Piper filled Zoey's cup and then poured a generous portion for herself. "Sticking to the comic book analogy, he and I are exactly like Batman and Catwoman, except he's the evil villain. I'm the superhero. Obviously."

Zoey snorted a laugh. "Obviously."

Now that Piper thought about it, Ethan had an awful lot in common with Bruce Wayne. They were both obscenely wealthy and prone to secrets. Although if memory served, Bruce Wayne hadn't walked away from the family fortune to become a forest ranger. And Ethan had shared his most important secret with her the night before.

Right before he'd rejected her.

Piper stirred her coffee with such vigor that it sloshed over the rim.

"If you say so, Catwoman. But I always got the impression that the caped crusader and his kittenish nemesis were secretly in love with each other." Zoey glanced at Ethan's image reflected back at them from all directions in the mirrored dance studio walls, and smirked. "Just saying."

Ethan had never set foot in a dance studio before. He'd also never had the misfortune to work with papier-mâché. Thus he was in no way prepared for how messy it was. Or fragrant. What difference did it make, though? The wet-paper smell should complement his stale-coffee-scented feet rather nicely.

"How's it going over here?" Piper asked, plopping down beside him with a stack of newspapers in her arms.

"Spectacular. I've made an entire tree." It looked more like a lopsided candy cane, but Posy had assured him that once it dried and they'd added paint and crepe paper leaves, it would be a masterpiece. He estimated the odds that she was merely patronizing him as fifty-fifty. "I'm running low on supplies, though."

"I noticed. I'm here to help." Piper grabbed a few sheets of newspaper from her stack. "Why don't I tear the paper into strips and hand them to you? We can be our own little assembly line."

"Sounds good." *And suspiciously helpful.*

He held out his hand and waited as she tore in half a page that he recognized from the *Yukon Reporter.* Two more rips and he saw his own likeness split right down the middle.

She smiled and handed him the piece with his dismembered forehead. "Here you go."

He took it from her and coated it with the gooey papier-mâché mixture. "You're enjoying this, aren't you?"

"A little." *Rip. Rip. Rip.*

There went his latest column—shredded into ribbons. "Would I be remiss in assuming that every newspaper in that pile of yours is a section with my writing in it?"

"No, you wouldn't." She smiled from ear to ear and tore this morning's front page—the one that had nearly gotten him fired—into ten thin strips.

He shook his head and muttered, "Nice."

Then the room swelled with scratchy vinyl piano music. Ethan looked up in time to see half a dozen little girls in black leotards and pale pink tights tiptoe inside and line up at the bar on the far side of the room. The floor-to-ceiling mirrors on every wall multiplied them fourfold. Everywhere Ethan looked he saw smiling, happy little girls.

Posy took her place in front of them. She'd changed into a long-sleeved black leotard and a wispy skirt the exact shade of pink cotton candy. "Good morning, girls. Let's start with pliés."

The students moved into a series of deep knee bends, and as Ethan watched them wobble on delicate candy-hued legs, his chest grew tight.

"Cute, aren't they?" Piper whispered.

"Yes." Ethan cleared his throat. He glanced from Posy to her, and only then did he notice Piper's wistful expression. He found it intriguing. She was so rarely unguarded. "Did you ever do this sort of thing?"

Piper blinked, and for a moment Ethan saw a sadness

in her eyes so profound that it grabbed him by the throat. She shook her head. "Ballet? Me? No."

"Never? No dance lessons when you were a kid?" At some point, she'd obviously devoted her life to animal rescue, but Piper was no tomboy. She was more of an enigma, and there was an undeniable grace in her movements. He could see her as a dancer. In another life, perhaps.

She grew quiet, and her systematic destruction of his newspaper column lost a little of its intensity. "No. Never."

"Let me guess. You grew up in a wolf den." It honestly wouldn't have surprised him.

Her next words, however, did. "Foster care, actually." *Foster care?*

All the while he'd been bemoaning his silver spoon existence, Piper had been in a foster home? He'd actually complained about his upbringing to her. In detail.

What must she have thought when he'd been spouting off all the extravagant particulars about his father's five-star hotel? *Six hundred and sixty-eight rooms. Thirty-one floors.*

He'd never felt like a bigger jerk in his life. And the chandeliers. Thank goodness he hadn't mentioned the ridiculous chandeliers. Still, he'd spoken about the rest of it with such contempt.

What had he been thinking? "You spent your childhood in a foster home?"

"*Homes*, actually. Plural." Her voice went hollow. Detached. It was almost as though she were talking about someone else, rather than herself. A perfect stranger. "I was almost four when my mom turned me over to the state. Not many people want to adopt kids that old, so I bounced around a bit."

Her mother had abandoned her? His heart hurt thinking about it, and yet it explained so much. No wonder she'd devoted her life to rescuing animals that were unwanted. No wonder...

He still had papier-mâché mess all over his hands, but he didn't care. He reached for her, and wove his fingers through hers. "I'm sorry, Piper."

"It's fine. Honest. It was a long time ago." She lifted a slender shoulder, but he could see the pain behind her emerald eyes. The distant look there had shifted and changed, as if she'd come back to herself. She was wholly present again. Beautiful, broken Piper Quinn.

The shift had occurred the moment he'd touched her, an observation that wasn't lost on Ethan.

"It might have been a long time ago, but I'm still sorry it happened." He gave her hand a squeeze, and the thing between them—attraction, affection, whatever it was—became harder to ignore. It pulsed there, demanding attention. The air in the studio shimmered with awareness.

The wolves made more sense now. He wasn't sure how or when it began, but she'd built a pack of her own. A family unshakable in its devotion.

Ethan almost understood it, but that didn't mean he had to like it. "I want you to know why I find the idea of this recital so upsetting."

"Okay." Piper's eyes grew as big as saucers. A line from *Little Red Riding Hood* snagged in his consciousness. *All the better to see you with, my dear.*

He swallowed and averted his gaze. But everywhere he looked, all those tiny ballerinas were reflected back at him in the mirrored walls. It was like gazing into a dream of what could have been. If only he'd been able to do something. If only.

"The victim of the bear attack was a little girl. Six years old. She'd been picking blueberries and wandered from her campsite. I found her just as she surprised a grizzly in some brush." Ethan still remembered it with picture-perfect clarity. The color of her dress. The ring of purple around her mouth from the berries she'd been eating. Her smile.

And then the sounds. Sounds more horrific than he could have imagined. He still heard them sometimes in his nightmares.

He swallowed. "I can't see something like that again, Piper." If he did, he'd never survive it. "I can't."

"You won't." Her grip on his hand tightened so much that his knuckles turned white.

But he didn't let go. Couldn't. Something was happening. In this room, this dancing hall of mirrors, they'd reached a critical moment. He knew with complete and utter certainty that they would either find a way to make peace with one another, or their impasse would become permanent. He'd shared his truth, and she'd shared hers. Where would they go from here?

The blood roared in his ears, distorting the balletic piano music. He wanted to believe her. He really did. But how could he? "You can't make that promise, Piper. Koko is a wolf."

It was the wrong thing to say.

Her grip on his hand loosened. "Yes, I can make that promise. It's not the same. You have to believe me."

Her pleading tone just about tore him in two. She was slipping through his fingers. He was slipping through hers. And there was nothing he could do to stop it.

"I wish I could." Maybe he'd waited too long to talk about what he'd seen. Maybe holding the words inside for so long made the memory cling that much harder. So hard that he couldn't seem to let it go, even though now he realized he almost wanted to. Maybe that's what he'd wanted all along.

"Koko isn't even going to be onstage with the girls. I'm bringing him out, on a lead, after they've done their part," she said.

"You do know the actual story of *Little Red Riding Hood*, don't you? Because it doesn't end well."

"We don't want to scare the kids, so we're changing the ending."

"Of course you are." Real life couldn't be so easily altered, though, could it? Real endings were permanent.

"Maybe you should spend some more one-on-one time with Koko," Piper was saying. "He's really a sweetheart. He was born and bred on a photo farm. Do you know what that is?"

Ethan did. "One of those places that breeds puppies and kittens and uses them as models for cute, fuzzy calendars. Yes, I'm familiar."

"When he grew out of the cute-and-fuzzy stage, they didn't know what to do with him. I guess they hadn't thought about what would happen once they had an actual wolf on their hands. They left him to starve in a Dumpster. He was barely alive when he was found. He spent over a month in a veterinary hospital before I volunteered to take him in."

Ethan sighed. "This is all very touching, Piper, but it still doesn't change my mind."

"I'm not telling you about Koko's history to get you to feel sorry for him. I'm telling you about it to let you know that he's different. He's spent his entire life with people. He knows humans better than he knows wolves. He's been handled and touched and socialized to be around us since the day he was born. He won't cause any trouble at the recital, even if one of the children accidentally got close to him." Piper swallowed. "Which won't happen. I won't let it. Please trust me."

Ethan held up a hand to stop her. It wasn't fair to let her go on thinking that she could convince him that having a wild animal anywhere near a group of children was a good idea.

Koko could have had the saddest sob story in the history of rescue animals and it wouldn't have made a lick of difference to Ethan. He was on the side of the children. Always. Forever. "Don't. I'm not going to change my mind about this. Nothing you can say will convince me."

"I see." She let go of his hand and stood. Shreds of his newspaper column fell from her lap and littered the floor. "We should go. I need to get back to the wolves."

His throat grew tight. "I know."

The wolves. It had come back around to the wolves. It always did. It always did and it always would.

Ethan just couldn't take it anymore. He couldn't stand watching her put herself in harm's way day in, day out any more than he could stomach the thought of a wolf at a children's dance recital. He'd tried not to care. He'd given it his best effort. No job was worth this. Not even a column on the front page of the newspaper.

He was finished.

To: Anna Plum aplum@theseattletribune.com
From: Ethan Hale ehale@alaskamail.com
Subject: Interview

Dear Ms. Plum,
My availability has changed. I can make a trip to Seattle at your earliest convenience.

I look forward to hearing from you and discussing the possibility of a position at your newspaper.
Best regards,
Ethan Hale

To: Ethan Hale ehale@alaskamail.com
From: Anna Plum aplum@theseattletribune.com
Subject: RE: Interview

Hello, Ethan,
Such great news!

I've taken the liberty of booking travel arrangements for you for the day after tomorrow. Your confirmation number and flight itinerary with Alaska Air are attached. A driver will pick you up in baggage claim upon your arrival.

I very much look forward to this opportunity to discuss your future at *The Seattle Tribune*. See you in two days!
Sincerely,
Anna Plum
Editor in Chief
The Seattle Tribune

Piper couldn't get out of the dance studio quickly enough. Something about all those little girls, coupled with Ethan holding her hand, was just too much to take.

She'd said too much. Obviously.

What had she been thinking, giving him all those details about her childhood? She rarely talked about being bounced around between foster homes. And she *never* talked about her mother. Ever.

Piper climbed into her car, took a deep breath and tried to wrap her mind about what had just happened. Ethan wasn't supposed to react the way he had. He wasn't supposed to be so...so compassionate. So sweet.

It might have been a long time ago, but I'm still sorry it happened.

She believed him. Everything about the way he'd looked at her, touched her, said that he cared. Very much.

And yet it still hadn't made a bit of difference.

She'd thought if he somehow knew how important the wolves were to her, if he understood *why*, that he would stop trying to undermine her at every turn. But he wasn't backing down. He never would. And now he was taking aim at Posy's dance recital.

Piper couldn't let him ruin things for Posy. Not after she'd been the one to suggest the *Little Red Riding Hood* theme to begin with. It was bad enough that her own wolf sanctuary was struggling to survive. She refused to take Posy down with her. If Ethan wrote something awful about the ballet recital, it would affect the dance studio just as much as the wolves.

And he would do it. She knew he would.

He could papier-mâché enough trees to cover the entire state of Alaska, but he'd volunteered for the recital committee for one reason and one reason only—to keep an eye on her. He was just waiting for the right moment to ruin everything.

But what really made the situation impossible to bear was the fact that she now knew why. Why he'd left the park service. Why he'd taken it upon himself to ruin every chance her wolves had for survival. She had her reasons, and he had his. Neither one of them was about to back down.

She wished she could despise him. She couldn't. Not anymore. He'd seen a child die. He'd tried to save her, and in his own way, he still was. How could Piper despise a man like that?

Her empty driveway was a sight for sore eyes once she'd made her way back to the sanctuary. She hadn't seen Ethan's SUV on the road, so she'd half assumed he'd be there waiting for her, seeing as he'd committed to following her every move.

She got out of the car and perched on her rock for a

few minutes, reveling in her solitude, the silence of the snowfall and the beauty of her wolves moving among the pines. She tried not to notice when Ethan failed to show up after ten minutes had passed, and then again when he still wasn't there after half an hour.

He was an abysmal failure as a stalker.

That was his problem, not hers, wasn't it? She pushed herself off the rock and headed to the cabin. Today was enrichment day on the wolves' schedule, so she had a little something special planned for them.

Wolves in the wild faced constant physical and mental challenges. From foraging for food, seeking out prey and avoiding hunters, to finding a mate and caring for a litter of pups, a wolf in its natural environment encountered stimulation at every turn. These beautiful animals were shaped by the world around them. Those that thrived survived.

Obviously, life for a rescue wolf living in captivity was vastly different from the daily struggle of surviving in the wild. Without the constant stimulation of their natural environment, wolves could become stressed. And stress could lead to harmful behaviors, such as pacing, illness, self-mutilation and even aggression. Piper was constantly coming up with new, innovative ways to keep her pack challenged, happy and smart. And today that particular task involved over one hundred fifty chicken broth ice cubes.

She opened her freezer and an ice tray came flying out. She caught it before it fell on her foot. A broken toe was all she needed to make this day complete.

Maybe she'd gotten a little overzealous with the wolf Popsicles. She'd gone through almost five gallons of chicken broth the night before. Enrichment was one of her favorite parts of her job, and every one of her wolves loved ice cubes. Even more so if they tasted like chicken.

She dumped a few trays' worth of ice cubes in a bucket and headed back outside. Much to her irritation, her heart gave a little pang when she still failed to spot Ethan's truck in the drive. Or anywhere in the vicinity.

She didn't miss him or anything. That would have been pathetic. He should be here for enrichment, though. It would give him something new and different to write in his column. Piper would have loved to read an article about her wolves playing with ice cubes rather than what dangerous, bloodthirsty predators they were.

She tossed a few chicken cubes over the fence of Tundra's enclosure. The white wolf leaped for them, twisting midair with the grace and elegance of a dancer. Tundra's teeth snapped shut with an audible bite. Then she landed on all fours, shook her woolly head and tossed the cube she'd caught back in the air. Piper smiled, watching her play, until she finally settled down in a white ball of fur on the snow with an ice cube between her front paws.

"Enjoy it, girl," Piper whispered as Tundra licked the cube with delicate swipes of her pink tongue.

By the time Piper got to the next pen, Shasta was prancing back and forth at the fence line with his ears pricked forward and his mouth open in a wide, wolfish grin. Shasta was never as polite as Tundra with his enrichment activities. He slammed against the fence on his back legs, gaze fixed on Piper's bucket. She pitched six chicken-broth ice cubes over the fence in rapid succession, all of which he somehow managed to catch. Shasta liked to swallow things whole. Ice cubes. Meat. Stray mittens on occasion.

"Goofball." Piper shook her head, grin fading. "Ethan doesn't know what he's missing, does he?"

Where *was* he, anyway? At least an hour had passed since she'd left Posy's ballet school. As pleasant as it was to be able to go about her business without him watching her every move, his absence was troublesome. It bothered her far more than it should have.

I'm just concerned for his safety. That's all. His car could have broken down.

Concerned for his safety. Right.

Ethan didn't want, or need, her concern. He had a cell phone. If that SUV where he liked to sleep so much had broken down, he could have called for help.

Unless he's been injured.

Piper hugged her empty bucket closer to her chest as she marched through the snowdrifts back toward the cabin. The snow was really coming down now, much thicker than earlier in the day. The curvy mountain road leading to the sanctuary had surely iced over, and it was typically one of the last streets in the city that road crews reached with salt and deicing chemicals. A car could slide clear off the mountain and no one would ever know.

She paused in front of her freezer again. What if something had happened? What if Ethan had indeed slid clear off the mountain?

Surely not.

She flung the freezer door open, even angrier with Ethan than usual. Which was pretty angry. How dare he make her worry like this? Didn't he know it was rude to announce his intention to stalk someone and then vanish off the face of the planet?

She reached for her cell phone and dialed Ethan's number while the air from the freezer cooled her face. She'd explain to him just how inconsiderate he was acting as soon as he answered.

But he didn't answer. The phone rang and rang, then went to voice mail. Piper didn't leave a message because, really, what could she say? *Where are you?* Right. And sound like a worried girlfriend, when that couldn't be further from the truth? No, thank you.

She pocketed her phone and went back to work, emptying ice trays into the bucket. She didn't have time to worry about Ethan's whereabouts. Didn't he know she had wolves to entertain?

She couldn't seem to shake the feeling that something was wrong, though. So when she'd filled the bucket, she tried his cell phone one more time.

Again, no answer.

Maybe it was time to call his editor. No, she couldn't. Ethan had already gotten in trouble with Lou for not knowing about her involvement with Posy's dance recital. Piper would *not* be directly responsible for Ethan losing his job. As much as she wanted him to stop insulting her life's work in the newspaper, getting him fired wasn't how she wanted things to end.

She slammed the freezer door, and her gaze landed on Tate Hudson's business card anchored to the brushed chrome with a magnet. Ethan had given it to her after the graffiti incident, with strict instructions to call if anything seemed amiss. Something seemed amiss, all right. Besides, Ethan and Tate were friends. They were probably living it up at the Northern Lights Inn coffee bar right that very minute.

Before she could change her mind, she dialed the number on the card.

"Tate Hudson."

This had seemed like a much better idea before he'd answered the phone. Maybe she should just hang up. But wait. He was a state trooper. Wouldn't he know exactly who'd hung up on him?

It was too late to back out now. She took a deep breath. "Hello, Tate. This is Piper from the wolf sanctuary."

"I hope everything is okay out there," he said, his professional tone laced with concern.

"I'm fine. The wolves are fine. No problem at all, except..." Gosh, this was humiliating. "Ethan."

"Ethan?" Tate laughed. "What's he done to upset you this time? It must be something really bad for you to call law enforcement."

"Funny." She rolled her eyes. The feud between her and Ethan was destined to go down in history, at least in the state of Alaska. "It's not like that. Listen, I'm not trying to alarm anyone unnecessarily. I know you and Ethan are friends, and it seems he's gone missing."

"Missing?"

"Yes." She gave him a rundown of the morning's events, assured him that, yes, she'd tried Ethan's cell phone and, no, he hadn't answered.

Tate promised to look into things. She hung up and reassured herself that she'd done the right thing. At least now she could continue enrichment with the wolves with a modicum of peace of mind.

Bucket in hand, she headed toward the cabin door. But just as she reached for the knob, a loud thump from outside shook the door in its frame.

Heart pounding, Piper took a giant backward step. She blew out a breath. "Ethan, you just about frightened me to death."

She knew he hadn't driven off the side of the mountain. He was too annoying to disappear entirely. She swung the door open, fully prepared to chastise him for worrying her enough that she'd called Tate and then for beating on her door like a caveman.

But Ethan wasn't the one standing on her front porch. Not even close.

Chapter Ten

Ethan tossed the last of his belongings into his duffel bag and zipped it closed. It felt as if a century had passed since he'd slept in his own bed. Now that he'd made the decision to quit his column, he couldn't wait to check out of the Northern Lights Inn. If he did so fast enough, he'd save the newspaper the cost of another night's stay.

Not that it mattered. Once Lou got wind of the fact that he'd walked away from the assignment, Ethan was sure to be out of a job. He'd had his chance, and he'd blown it. He'd broken the cardinal rule of journalism. He'd failed to maintain his objectivity. Worse than that, he'd become personally involved. With the woman as much as the story.

At least he'd managed not to kiss her.

He stood for a moment, thoughts snagged on the notion of kissing Piper Quinn, until someone knocked on the door to his room.

"Ethan, you in there? Open up. It's Tate."

What now?

Ethan reached for the door and swung it open. "Sorry, but I'm not really in the mood for visitors."

"I'm not visiting. I'm here on business." Tate's hand

rested casually on the radio in his holster as if to emphasize his point.

Ethan's brow furrowed. "What kind of business?"

"Missing person business."

A missing person? In Aurora? The one time someone had been reported missing in town it had been a retired fisherman who'd wandered away one late summer morning from his room at the assisted living facility. Tate had located him less than an hour later on the banks of the river, fishing pole in hand and picnic basket at his feet.

"Who's missing?" Ethan asked.

"You are."

"No, I'm not. I'm standing right here."

"I see that. Listen, you may want to call your boss."

"Lou?" Ethan hadn't even had a chance to quit yet, and already Lou was hunting him down? Not a good sign. At all. "How does he know I'm not at the wolf sanctuary?"

"Not Lou." Tate shook his head. "Piper. She called the station and reported you missing."

"What?" Unbelievable.

Tate sank into the hotel room's lone armchair. "Yep. And might I add that it's the first time anyone's called in because they were worried about their 'stalker.'"

"I was *not* stalking her. I was doing my job."

"Was doing your job?" Tate frowned. "What's exactly going on here, friend?"

Ethan blew out a breath. "Nothing. I'm quitting. That's all."

"You're quitting your job? Does this mean you got the position at the paper in Seattle?"

Did they have to do this right now? Ethan had never been less in the mood for a heart-to-heart. "Not my job. Just my column. And Lou doesn't know I'm giving it up yet, so I'd be grateful if you could keep a lid on it."

"You're quitting your column? The one on the *front page* of the newspaper?" Tate shook his head. "I was less worried when I thought you were a missing person who'd also been accused of stalking."

"I'm fine. It just got…"

Tate raised his brows.

"…personal." Ethan picked up the duffel bag and hauled it onto his shoulder. "And that's all I'm going to say about it."

Tate stood. "Okay. But give Piper a call, would you? So she knows you're alive and well."

Alive and well.

Ethan didn't feel either.

"Fine." Piper deserved an explanation, and the news would probably be better coming from him than from Lou.

She'd be hurt. And angry. But she'd have to agree that this was better for both of them. Maybe Lou would keep the column going. Maybe he'd send another reporter to the sanctuary, one more sympathetic to her cause. That's what she'd wanted all along. She'd definitely be happier if someone different was assigned to the story.

The idea didn't sit well with Ethan.

Before he could process a feeling that felt altogether too much like jealousy, the portable radio in Tate's holster buzzed to life.

"Dispatch to Captain Hudson. Nine-one-one. Are you in? Over."

"What now?" Tate shot a worried glance at Ethan and reached for the radio. "This is Hudson. Go ahead."

"We've got a possible hostage situation just outside the town limits. Repeat, a possible hostage situation. Over."

A hostage situation?

Aurora had never experienced anything remotely as

dangerous as a hostage crisis. Surely there'd been a mistake. Some kind of misunderstanding.

Ethan tossed his duffel on the bed. He'd follow Tate to wherever the thing was going down. Maybe he'd get a big enough scoop for the newspaper that Lou would keep him onboard.

"I copy. On my way. What's the 20?" Tate was already out the door, halfway down the hall, before he even knew where he was headed.

Ethan matched his stride, step for step. Everything was happening in a blurry rush of alarm.

Then the dispatcher spoke again, and the world came to a screeching halt. "One-eleven Chugach Scenic Road. Do you copy?"

Piper's address.

Tate barked something into the radio, but Ethan didn't make out the words. His head buzzed with white noise. Sickness rose to the back of his throat.

How had this happened?

He should have been there. He was *supposed* to be there right now. Was this some kind of cosmic joke? He couldn't be responsible for losing someone. Not again.

And not Piper.

"Ethan!" Tate snapped.

Ethan had almost forgotten Tate was even there. He'd been concentrating on nothing but running. Moving. Getting to Piper as fast as he could. Before it was too late.

They pushed through the revolving door of the inn, out into the snow and cold. Ethan's SUV was parked close by, but Tate rapped on the hood of the police cruiser that occupied the spot nearest the hotel.

"Get in. You can ride in the squad car with me."

Ethan swung open the door and climbed into the passenger seat. Tate pulled out of the parking space, sirens blaring, before Ethan even had his seat belt buckled.

He was grateful for the ride, grateful for Tate's siren and flashing red lights. But the wolf sanctuary was halfway up the mountain, a fact that had nagged at Ethan since the moment he'd first set foot on Piper's property. The trip up the mountainous winding road would take a minimum of fifteen minutes, regardless of how fast Tate drove or how loud his sirens blared. It was a simple matter of physics. And that was the absolute best-case scenario. Ethan didn't want to contemplate the worst.

A lot could happen in fifteen minutes. A life could be lost in half as much time.

The bear attack had occurred in under six minutes. He'd made a call on his radio at 7:02 p.m., the moment he'd spotted the missing girl. By 7:08 p.m., she was gone. Those had been the longest six minutes of Ethan's life. Until now.

Tate handed Ethan his cell phone. "Why don't you dial Dispatch on speaker, and see if they can give us any additional information?"

Ethan had the dispatch officer on the line in less than ten seconds. "Tate? Are you on your way up to the wolf sanctuary?"

"Yes, and I've got Ethan here with me." The tires screeched as he maneuvered the car around a bend in the road. "Can you give us a rundown of the call?"

"Sure. Piper called in and asked for you at exactly 10:28 a.m." Ten minutes ago. Ethan closed his eyes, but all he could see was the word *Killers* painted on the side of her cabin. He opened his eyes and blinked a few times, but could no longer seem to see anything else. How could he have left her there alone? She'd been threatened, and he'd turned his back on the vow he'd made to himself to keep her safe.

The dispatcher continued. "She asked for you, Tate, and said she was trapped inside her cabin because someone was holding her hostage. She mentioned a name, but it was unintelligible. When I asked her to repeat it, the line went dead. I've tried calling back multiple times, but her number goes straight to voice mail."

Ethan and Tate exchanged a glance. This didn't sound good. Not at all.

"The strange thing about the call was how calm she sounded. Very composed in light of the circumstances."

Ethan wished he could take solace in this news, but he couldn't. Every one of Piper's wolves outweighed her, and she let them crawl all over her every day. Sometimes he wondered if the woman had the good sense to know when to be afraid.

Tate gunned the accelerator as the cruiser headed up a steep incline. "Thanks. We're turning off the main road and should be there in an under a minute. Send for backup if you haven't already."

"All cars are already en route."

"Excellent." Tate nodded, and Ethan ended the call.

Every state trooper in the vicinity was on his or her way to Piper's property. Outside the police cruiser, the snow was coming down so thick and white that it looked like the end of the world was at hand. This wasn't a nightmare. It wasn't a product of Ethan's overactive imagination. This was real.

God, not again. Please not again.

He would have promised everything. Anything. Just please not again.

"Seriously? You're just going to stand there in my doorway and keep me trapped in here?" Piper sighed.

She was beginning to warm up to her captor. Sure,

she'd been startled at first. Maybe even a little afraid. But once she'd had a chance to catch her breath and assess the situation, she realized he wasn't so bad. He was actually kinda cute.

In a Rudolph sort of way.

"So you're the infamous Palmer." She inched closer to the massive reindeer looming in the entryway to her cabin. When she'd opened the front door, oblivious to what waited for her on the other side, he'd taken the liberty of walking right up to her. Apparently, he was an in-your-face sort of reindeer. Now here he stood, halfway in and halfway out of her home. He'd nearly toppled the vase of flowers that Caleb had picked for her.

He wasn't wearing a name tag or anything, but it had to be him. Palmer. The reindeer she'd heard so much about who had a penchant for escaping the confines of the neighboring reindeer farm. The reindeer that Ethan had been so worried about becoming snack food for her wolves. Well, the wolves were all exactly where they were supposed to be at the moment, weren't they? It was Palmer's behavior that bordered on assault.

Oh, the irony.

"Has anyone ever told you that you're rather forward?"

Palmer grunted in response. He was awfully cute for a criminal—with long, fluttering eyelashes and a cute white ring around one of his dark eyes. But goodness, he was big. If he managed to force his way completely inside the cabin, she'd have an enormous mess on her hands.

She stood her ground, less than a foot away from his colossal caribou face, and prayed he would just stay there until help arrived.

Zoey had been the first person that Piper called. Palmer belonged to her, after all. Apparently, she was accustomed to getting these sorts of calls. When her number rolled straight to voice mail, Piper remembered that Zoey was scheduled to fly up to Anchorage on a mail run in her plane today. In addition to running the reindeer farm with her husband, she was also Aurora's chief charter pilot.

With Zoey unavailable, Piper wasn't quite sure what to do. So she'd called 911. Because she was pretty sure being pinned inside your home by a reindeer was an actual emergency, albeit a uniquely Alaskan one.

At least she'd managed to get her information rattled off to the police dispatcher before her cell phone had died. She wasn't about to turn her back on Palmer long enough to carry her phone to its charger in the kitchen. By the time she got it plugged in, he probably would have stomped all the way to her bedroom and tucked himself into her feather bed.

"The police are on their way, so now's the time to make a break for it if you don't want another infraction on your already notorious arrest record."

Palmer lowered his head and let out a throaty rattling noise. Piper had no idea whether or not such reindeer behavior was normal, or what it meant. She'd been a little too busy communing with wolves for the past ten years to brush up on reindeer vocalizations.

She glanced at the bucket at her feet. Maybe she should offer him one of the chicken-broth ice cubes. Or were reindeer vegetarian? She was pretty sure they were.

She sighed. Again.

When would the police arrive, and what was she supposed to do in the meantime with a reindeer halfway in her living room?

It took Ethan a minute to make sense of what he saw when the cruiser barreled onto Piper's property. Through the blinding snow, all he could make out was something dark in the doorway to the cabin. Much to Tate's annoyance, Ethan jumped out of the car before it came to a complete stop. Once outside, he recognized that the bulky thing obstructing Piper's door was an animal. His heart stopped beating as a series of horrific pictures flashed in his head. Wolves. Blood. Piper's lifeless body.

Then he got closer and realized he wasn't gazing at a wolf at all.

"You've got to be kidding me," Tate muttered as he reached his side. "Palmer."

"Looks that way." Ethan allowed himself to breathe again. He inhaled a shaky breath and tried to still the tremble in his hands.

It took a minute for his body to catch up with his mind. Piper wasn't being held captive by a dangerous criminal, after all. Nor was she being torn limb from limb by one of her precious wolves. The source of her trouble was just a silly reindeer. This kind of thing happened all the time. It did in Palmer's stomping ground, anyway.

Everything was okay.

Tate gave him a nudge. "You all right, man? You're white as a sheet."

"Fine." Ethan's throat closed like a fist. "I'm fine."

"I need to radio this in, so Dispatch can cancel the call for backup. And I'll go grab the carrots out of my trunk. See if you can check on Piper, okay?"

"You keep carrots in the trunk of your squad car?" This struck Ethan as particularly absurd. He probably would have laughed if he wasn't still shaking off the physical effects of panic.

"They're regulation now for every officer in Aurora, thanks to the town wanderer over there." Tate nodded toward Palmer's massive backside protruding from the entrance to Piper's cabin. "I've got a whole bag of them. Be right back."

Ethan shook his head and gave in to the smile working its way to his mouth. Hostage-taking reindeer. Carrot-wielding law enforcement officers.

Only in Alaska.

He'd miss things like these once he moved to Seattle, he realized. Alaska was like no place else on the planet. Peculiar. Wild. Free. Which was why he'd wanted to come here in the first place. Ultimately, though, Alaska's adventuresome spirit was precisely why he wanted to leave. The police in the Lower 48 didn't carry carrots. But grizzly bears didn't walk down the sidewalks, either.

That mattered. Didn't it?

Ethan trudged toward Piper's cabin through the shin-deep snow. He was getting ahead of himself. Just because he was scheduled to fly down to Seattle the day after tomorrow didn't mean he was moving there permanently. He didn't even have the job at *The Seattle Tribune.* Yet.

"Hey there, you mischief maker." Ethan didn't want to startle the reindeer, so he rested a calming hand on the animal's flank.

Palmer's hide quivered under the touch. Beneath its fine dusting of snow, the reindeer's body was warm, soft, pulsing with life. Ethan had a memory of feeding caribou apples from the palms of his hands back in Denali. Of the velvety softness of their antlers in springtime. Their soft footfalls in the snow.

"Hello? Is someone there?" Piper called from inside the cabin.

She sounded perfectly fine. Unharmed. Safe. But for some odd reason, hearing her voice caused Ethan's chest to tighten into a raw, aching knot. "It's me."

"Ethan!" The relief in her tone did nothing to lessen the ache. "You're okay. Good."

"*I'm* okay?" He couldn't help but laugh. "You called 911, yet you were worried about *my* safety? Might I remind you that there's a reindeer protruding from your house?"

"Ha. Ha." He could practically hear her eyes rolling. "Wait a minute. Why are you here? Now? I expected you hours ago."

He swallowed. "Wouldn't you rather talk about that after we get the hostage situation taken care of?"

"We? Who else is out there? I can't see a thing past Rudolph."

Tate reappeared gripping a fistful of carrots. "Hello, Piper. It's Tate Hudson. Are you okay?"

"Yes. Absolutely." She didn't sound quite as concerned as one might expect under the circumstances. Leave it to Piper to take a home invasion by a reindeer in stride. "How do we get him out of here, though? It's been twenty minutes and he hasn't budged. I think he might have even fallen asleep standing up for a minute or two."

A second set of tires rumbled through the snow. Ethan turned to see Zoey Wynn hop out of her little car and come barreling toward them. "Oh, no! Not again. Palmer, you naughty, naughty boy."

Ethan grinned. "Zoey, nice to see you."

Her gaze flitted back and forth between him and Tate. "Great. The cavalry has already arrived. I suppose this means I'm racking up another citation for animal at large."

Tate shrugged. "That depends. Piper hasn't indicated whether or not she'd like to press charges."

"Of course I don't," she called from inside. "But it would be really nice if you could get this beast out of my house."

"Deal." Zoey shot Tate a triumphant grin. "I'm so sorry

I didn't pick up when you phoned, Piper. I had my mail run to Anchorage, and then at the last minute I got a call to pick up a businessman in Juneau. Some government official. I got your voice mail and headed straight over here. Just let me go grab some treats. I think I've got some in the car."

Tate waved a carrot at her. "No need."

"Super. I'll let you coax him out of there, since Palmer knows you as well as anyone by now." Zoey took a backward step out of the way.

Ethan followed.

"I suppose you're going to write about this in the newspaper." Zoey lifted a brow. *"Again."*

Ethan pulled his cell phone out of his pocket and snapped a few photos. "Come on, Zoey. No hard feelings. You know it's my solemn duty to report the news. And this—" he nodded toward Palmer's woolly backside "—is certainly news."

Zoey sighed. "I don't suppose you could try to put a positive spin on it?"

On a reindeer barging into someone's home? "That wouldn't be very impartial of me, now, would it?"

Zoey snort-laughed right in his face. "I didn't realize you were still pretending to be impartial."

"What's that supposed to mean?"

"I think you know." She pinned him with a knowing glare. "You should ease up on Piper, Ethan. I've been getting to know her through our work on the recital planning committee. She seems like a very caring person. She's not out to hurt anyone, and neither are her wolves…in case you haven't noticed."

She gave him a parting wave and joined Tate, who'd thus far managed to lure Palmer about three feet away from Piper's door. Zoey looped her arm around the reindeer's thick neck and cooed soothing words to him as Tate guided him in the direction of the reindeer farm.

Ethan stood watching them for a moment, thoughts whirling in his mind like snowflakes. Had he really been blatantly unfair to Piper in his column? Granted, he'd made his opinion on the presence of a wolf sanctuary in Aurora more than clear. But his points had been perfectly valid. Wolves were predators, and therefore presented a threat. Everything he'd written rang true.

It no longer mattered now, anyway. He'd had enough. Piper could live all alone with a bunch of wolves, and he wouldn't have anything else to say about it. Because he was quitting.

Definitely.

Probably.

"Ethan." Piper stepped outside, and the sight of her filled him with such immediate, overwhelming relief that he forgot about his column.

He forgot about Seattle and hotels and all the reasons he had for leaving Alaska. He even forgot about the wolves.

He'd thought he'd lost her. She'd been perfectly fine all along, but for nearly twenty endless minutes, Ethan had envisioned the worst. For the entire drive up the mountain, he'd bargained with God. He'd begged. He'd pleaded. But even as he'd prayed, even as he'd cast those desperate pleas up above, he'd never expected God to listen. To care. Why would He?

But He did.

Thank You, God. Thank You.

"Piper." He swept the waves of windblown curls from her eyes, and something moved in his chest, taking the ache that had formed there to a new and foreign place. Where pain blurred with pleasure.

She was beautiful. So beautiful that it hurt to gaze into her radiant eyes. Eyes like the auroras. She was beautiful. She was alive. And she was here.

"I thought…" He shook his head. He didn't want to say it. Didn't want to give voice to the fears that had so consumed him, lest they become real.

But he'd moved beyond the ability to choose his words or his actions. His hands had somehow found their way into her hair, and the pad of his thumb was brushing across the tender swell of her bottom lip, where he wanted most to kiss her. He didn't think he'd ever wanted anything more in his entire, messed-up life.

"You thought what?" Her voice had dropped to a tremulous whisper, and Ethan could see a thousand questions shining in her eyes. Questions that he wasn't sure how to answer.

Because he didn't know what was happening between them. He didn't know why he couldn't walk away from this place, or from her. He just knew he couldn't. He couldn't quit his column. He'd stay here for the remainder of the two weeks, as promised. He would still go to Seattle for his interview, but when it was over, he'd turn around and come right back.

He wasn't finished here. Not now. Not yet. Not until…

"Never mind what I thought," he growled.

Then he lifted her chin with a tender touch of his fingertips and lowered his mouth to hers.

She let out a tiny gasp of surprise, but in the span of a heartbeat, she melted into him. Her arms wrapped around his neck, and her fingertips played at the back of his hair. And she was so impossibly soft and warm that Ethan could only compare holding her to the feeling he got when he watched the early morning fog wrap itself around the mountains in a diaphanous caress.

He deepened the kiss, wanting more, needing more. And found that somehow she tasted of sweet sorrow, shadowy forests and meandering paths to places Ethan had long forgotten. Of nights dreaming under frozen diamond stars and the wild wolf moon. Of Arctic kaleidoscope skies, winter wind on his face and untouched snowfields at dawn. Of nature. Of Alaska.

Of life.

And for one wondrous moment, Ethan's brutal, meandering heart came to a place of healing.

Chapter Eleven

Piper didn't want to open her eyes. She feared if she did, she would find herself in a dream. Because Ethan Hale couldn't possibly be kissing her like this. As if she were a priceless treasure. As if he'd seen every part of her—the best, the worst and all myriad of shades in between—and he still wanted her. He still cared.

She'd never even told Stephen about her childhood. He'd thought her parents had died. And for all she knew, that was true. She'd never trusted him with the entirety of her truth, though. Nor anyone else. She didn't want sympathy or to be seen as some pathetic orphan. Announcing that she'd been abandoned as a child and grown up in foster care almost felt like waving a red flag.

Approach with caution.

Broken.

Unlovable.

She wasn't sure why she'd shared so much with Ethan. At the time she'd told herself that it was simply a matter of reciprocation. He'd opened up to her about his childhood, so she'd done the same. He'd even told her about what had happened to him in Denali, and clearly, that wasn't something he shared with just anyone.

So why had he chosen to expose such a secret part of himself to her? She wished she knew. Because she had a feeling that whatever the reason, it was the same one that had prompted her to reveal herself to him.

Now here they stood, souls and childhoods bared, kissing one another's pasts as surely as their cold, soft lips. It was a kiss that felt as though it could close old wounds, and leave tenderness in place of scars. Dreamlike. Wondrous. And overwhelming, because mended hearts were fragile and all too easily broken.

Her eyelashes fluttered open at last, and he was still there, standing against the backdrop of the rugged Chugach range. And he looked so perfect, so at home among those craggy rocks and the cool blue spruce trees that she could have cried. She wasn't dreaming. Ethan was real. She wanted to touch the chiseled planes of his face, just to be sure. She wanted him to whisper secrets in her ear and tell her all the things he'd never told anyone else. Most of all, she wanted him to kiss her again.

But somewhere beneath the dreamy haze of first-kiss euphoria, something felt out of place. Wrong. Like a wisp of black smoke in a clear blue sky.

Ethan. Here. Now.

It didn't make sense. None of this did.

He smiled down at her, and she asked the question she could no longer ignore. "Where were you? What happened to not letting me out of your sight? I thought something had happened to you."

Could she sound any more pathetic? Or, heaven forbid, lovesick? Why would she sound lovesick? She didn't love him. Of course she didn't.

Except sometimes when he was around, she experienced a strange weightless sensation. Like falling, almost.

Oh, no.

You do not *love him. You don't love him, and you surely don't need him. You have the wolves. You don't need anyone, least of all* him.

"You were worried about me." The corner of his mouth twitched into a bemused half grin.

Okay, so she'd been worried. But only a little. "No, I wasn't."

"Yes, you were." He narrowed his gaze, and the gray of his eyes rumbled through her like thunder over the Bering Sea. "You were worried about me. That's not all. I dare say you also missed me."

And she hated herself because he was right. She'd been worried. She'd even managed to convince herself that he'd driven off the side of the mountain. She'd been so concerned about him that she'd actually called the state trooper. Who did that? Husbands and wives, that's who.

Piper felt sick all of a sudden.

Even worse than worrying about him, she'd also missed him. Not because Caleb was still sick and the chores around the sanctuary weren't getting done. Not because Ethan had announced his plans to shadow her every move. Not even because of the silly chicken-broth ice cubes. She simply missed him. Ethan. Because she didn't loathe him quite as much as she thought she did. She actually liked him. Quite a lot. And despite all the overwhelming evidence to the contrary, she felt as if he understood her. Somewhere beneath his rough and wounded exterior beat a heart that moved to the rhythm of mountain snowfalls and winding forest trails. To the tune of God's creation.

But that was impossible.

And she didn't want to feel that way. Not about anyone. Certainly not about Ethan.

He slid his hands around her waist and pulled her close until she was once again enveloped in his comforting scent of pine and wood smoke. His old life still clung to him in more ways than he knew. Piper felt herself yielding again. Her face tipped up toward his, and her lips parted, ever so slightly, ever so ready for him to kiss her again.

Snow drifted down from a sky the color of glaciers in springtime and surrounded them in a feathery embrace. The wind whispered through the lonely forest, and it sounded almost like a sigh. Ethan bowed his head, and it would have been so easy to let her eyes flutter shut and forget everything else but this breathtaking moment and this maddening man.

His lips were a murmur away, and she could feel the warm promise of his breath against her skin. She rose on yearning tiptoe…

Stop. Something isn't right.

She opened her eyes. This time, to reality. "Wait."

Ethan straightened. "Wait?"

"Yes. Wait." Piper planted her hands on his chest and pushed him away. Or tried, anyway. His chest was remarkably solid, and try as she might, he didn't budge. "You weren't coming back, were you?"

He hesitated just long enough for her to know that she'd hit the nail right on its proverbial head.

"Don't lie to me, Ethan." If there was one thing she couldn't tolerate, it was dishonesty. Not after Stephen. "You know how I hate that."

"Okay. I wasn't planning on coming back. I thought it was for the best." His eyes grew dark, serious. Full of intention. "I was wrong."

"I knew it." She pushed him away again, and this time he let her.

"Piper."

"Don't. Don't say my name like that, like you care."

He reached for her, and she swatted his hand away. How

could she have let him kiss her like that? How could she have kissed him back?

She'd been doing just fine here on her quiet mountain with her wolves before he'd come along. How could she have trusted him, even for a minute?

"I knew it." She shook her head. "You were going to just walk away without a word. Not even a goodbye."

"You know it's more complicated than that, Piper." He raked a desperate hand through his hair. "I have a past, and so do you. Those pasts matter. They shape the way we feel and think."

This still didn't explain why he'd planned to up and disappear, leaving her to wonder where he'd gone. "And?"

He planted his hands on his hips and looked away, toward the wolf pens. "And it didn't seem right to keep trying to shut this place down. Not after what you told me this morning."

A shiver coursed through her. She suddenly felt cold and very exposed. "Then don't. Please don't."

"But that's exactly what I'll keep doing if I stay here. As much as I care about you...maybe *because* I care about you...I haven't changed my mind about the wolves." He turned his back on the enclosures.

Over his shoulder, Piper could see Koko's dark form among the hemlocks, his copper eyes trained on her. As always. "But you're wrong. Don't you see? I even had a reindeer here for half the day, and the wolves were just fine. Nothing bad happened."

"This time." An angry knot formed in Ethan's jaw. "Do you have any idea how I felt when Tate got the emergency dispatch on his radio? Think, Piper. Think for a minute about what I thought I'd find by the time I got to you. I was half out of my mind with terror."

"I'm sorry." Why did she feel she should apologize?

She'd done nothing wrong. Nothing at all. He should be the one apologizing to her. "But are you telling me that if Palmer hadn't wandered away from home and barged through my front door, you wouldn't be standing here right now?"

Ethan grew very still, very quiet. Piper knew the answer before he even said it. "Yes, that's right. But…"

"But nothing." She held up a hand. She couldn't listen to this anymore. Not a single word. "You were right. You don't belong here. You should have never come back. I wish you hadn't, but not as much as I wish you hadn't kissed me."

The knot in Ethan's jaw hardened. "Don't say that."

"Too late. I already did. You should know, better than anyone, that words can never be unsaid." That's what had started this entire mess. Words.

She was sick of words. Humans were the only species capable of using language. And what did they do? They used their words to lie and hurt one another. Over and over again. She couldn't take it anymore. At least wolves were honest.

They communicated with their bodies. They could show how they felt by how they carried their tails, moved their eyes or showed their teeth. To Piper, it seemed far more effective than words.

"Goodbye, Ethan." She strode past him and shut herself back inside the cabin.

She didn't know whether he left or stayed to tend to the wolves, and she really didn't care. Whatever he decided, she knew she could no longer pin her hopes on anything he wrote. His words were meaningless.

But his kiss…

A kiss like that couldn't lie.

Or could it?

* * *

To: Anna Plum aplum@theseattletribune.com
From: Ethan Hale ehale@alaskamail.com
Subject: Travel arrangements

Dear Ms. Plum,
Thank you for making the necessary travel arrangements
for my trip to Seattle. I'm in receipt of the itinerary and
ticketing information.

I look forward to meeting you tomorrow afternoon and
exploring a future with *The Seattle Tribune*.
Best regards,
Ethan Hale

"Could you have used a less flattering photograph of my
backside?" Tate tossed the morning edition of the *Yukon
Reporter* on the coffee bar and frowned at the picture
splashed across the front page.

"What can I say? Pictures don't lie." Ethan swiveled on
his bar stool. Another morning at the Northern Lights Inn
meant another morning drinking his coffee in the shadow
of a grizzly bear. Marvelous. "Besides, the readers aren't
looking at you. They're looking at Palmer, whose backside
is a fair bit larger than yours, I might add."

"Thanks. I guess." Tate eyed Ethan over the rim of his
coffee cup. "Nice column, by the way. What happened to
quitting?"

"I changed my mind." Ethan fixed his gaze out the window, toward the frozen lake that served as the landing strip
for Aurora's one and only airport. This time tomorrow, he
was scheduled to be on a plane to Seattle. He still hadn't
quite worked out how that was going to fit into his schedule, but he'd make it work. He had to. A chance like that
didn't come around more than once.

Still, he wasn't giving up the wolf column. He'd meant what he'd said to Piper. The decision to quit had been a mistake. He knew that now. Leaving without saying good-bye would have been cruel. She was right. About every-thing. Well, almost everything.

You don't belong here. You should have never come back. I wish you hadn't, but not as much as I wish you hadn't kissed me.

He might not belong on the wolf sanctuary—in fact, he was certain he didn't—but that kiss hadn't been a mis-take. He wasn't kidding himself. Nothing could come of him and Piper. And nothing would. With any luck, he'd be moving to Seattle within ten days.

But kissing her was something he'd never regret.

"What changed your mind?" Tate slid him a sideways glance.

Ethan shrugged. "Not any one thing."

His friend slammed his coffee cup down on the counter, and a generous portion of Gold Rush blend sloshed over the edge. "That might be the biggest lie I've ever heard."

Ethan gritted his teeth. "Drop it, Tate."

"No."

"Excuse me?"

"I said no. I will not drop it." He leaned forward, eyes shining with concern. "You've been avoiding talking about any of this with me for over a week now. I'm not letting you get away with it again. Every time I bring up the news-paper, moving to Seattle, the wolf sanctuary or the wolf woman—especially the wolf woman—you freeze up on me. Do you honestly think I haven't noticed?"

Ethan pinned him with a glare. "First off, what kind of law enforcement officer would you be if you didn't notice behavior patterns? And apparently, I've developed such a pattern. Second, don't call her the *wolf woman*. She has a name."

"So this is about Piper." Tate's mouth curved into a grin. "I knew it."

Ethan didn't bother denying it. Tate obviously wasn't going to drop it this time.

"Look, I'm not just telling you what I'm about to say as your friend. I'm saying it as someone who's seen you struggle to keep putting one foot in front of the other for the past five years." Tate held up every finger of his left hand as a visual. "Five years is a long time. I've been by your side, holding my tongue, first when you watched your wife walk out the door, then when you stopped going to church, stopped talking to people and in general stopped *living*."

"Susan was a mistake." Ethan shook his head. "From the very beginning."

"No argument here. I know that." Tate nodded. "Do you know *how* I know that?"

"How?"

"Because the entire time you were married, I never saw you look at Susan the way you look at Piper."

Ethan leveled his gaze at Tate. "It's not like that."

"Isn't it?" He rolled his eyes. "You're not fooling anybody. Everyone in the entire state of Alaska can see that you're crazy about one another."

"You're wrong. All of you."

"I saw the kiss."

Ethan stared into his coffee.

"I wasn't spying on you or anything. Zoey and I were right there. Palmer, too. Even the blasted reindeer could see that something special was happening between you and Piper." Tate let out a chuckle. "It was quite a kiss. I'm guessing it could be seen from space."

"It was a moment, okay? A rather exceptional moment,

but that's all. Nothing more. It will never be anything more. It can't." *Because I can't. And I don't think she can, either.*

"Don't screw this up, Ethan. If you do, you'll regret it for the rest of your life. And I know you have a healthy respect for regret." Tate stared pointedly at the stuffed grizzly bear propped in the corner.

Ethan had never hated that monstrosity so much in his life. "It's not that easy, Tate. I oppose everything she believes in."

Tate shrugged. "So stop."

"That's your advice? Just stop?" Disappointment coursed through him, and he wasn't even sure why. He'd already spun every possibility round and round in his head, and it kept coming down to the wolves. Every time. The wolves weren't going anywhere. They were a fundamental part of who Piper was.

And that was a problem.

"Yes, stop fighting with her," Tate said, as if it were a simple matter of choice. "Let it go, man. It's time."

He didn't understand. How could he? "It's not that easy."

Even if it were, even if Ethan could somehow have a change of heart—and he didn't see how that would ever be in the realm of possibility—Piper had already told him in no uncertain terms that she wasn't interested. She regretted the kiss. She probably regretted anything and everything to do with him. She'd basically ordered him to stay away from her and her wolves. Romance couldn't be further from the picture. Ethan was already prepared to do battle with her when he showed up at the sanctuary later this morning to do his job.

But you're not letting that stop you, are you? You're still going.

Tate's radio crackled to life. He was needed at the scene of a minor accident.

"You say it's not that easy. Things worth fighting for rarely are." He slid off his bar stool and gave Ethan a final sad smile. "Think about it."

When Piper heard a knock on her front door early in the morning the day after Palmer's fateful visit, she approached the situation with caution. The last thing she needed was another home invasion instigated by a reindeer, followed by a dashing rescue from Ethan and the police. No, thank you.

She opened the door just wide enough to let in a sliver of daylight.

"Don't worry. I'm not a wild animal." On the opposite side of the door, Zoey smiled and held up a plate of cinnamon rolls. The sweet smell of sugar and icing wafted inside. "I've brought a peace offering. I figured I owed you one for not pressing charges against my renegade reindeer."

"Come in." Piper swung the door the rest of the way open and motioned for her to step inside. "A peace offering really wasn't necessary. But thank you, because goodness, those smell divine."

"It was definitely necessary. You have no idea how many citations Palmer has managed to rack up. He's quite the criminal."

"So I've heard." Piper cleared the books and stacks of paper from her kitchen table and made a place for Zoey's platter. "Sorry about the mess. I've been working on an application for a grant from the National Nature Conservatory, and the paperwork has pretty much taken over the cabin."

"A grant application? That sounds like a lot of work."

"It was. Believe me. I barely got it in on time." No thanks to Ethan. "Hopefully, the NNC will be willing to at least send someone out here for an inspection."

"Best of luck," Zoey said.

"Thanks. I'm kind of desperate, actually. Now that Ethan's column has everyone afraid to sign up for a guided tour, all my hopes for funding are pinned on that grant. If it doesn't come through, I'm not sure what I'm going to do."

"There's always the dance recital. I think the wolf will be a big hit. I'm sure your tours will pick back up once everyone gets a chance to meet Koko."

Maybe. If Ethan doesn't somehow ruin that, too.

"I hope so." If the grant didn't come through, the recital would be her absolute last resort. "Koko's a natural charmer. That's for sure. He was extra cute this morning when I did my rounds, acting like a goof ball and chasing his tail. Wolves don't typically behave that way. But Koko is special."

"See? Don't worry. He'll charm the pants off everyone at the recital, and you'll be so busy with tours that you won't know what to do with yourself."

Piper hoped so. She really did. She was trying to imagine what such a sway in public sentiment would feel like when Zoey motioned toward the vase of purple blooms in the center of the table. "What gorgeous flowers. Ethan didn't give those to you, did he?"

"Ha!" The notion was beyond laughable. Although, really, if anyone should be bringing her a peace offering, it was him. *Sorry I humiliated you in the newspaper. Sorry I crushed your dreams. Sorry I kissed you within an inch of your life and then admitted I never planned on seeing you again.* There weren't enough flowers in all of Alaska to cover those apologies. "Caleb picked those for me. He found them growing in the snow. Can you believe that? He's such a sweet kid."

"Is he here today?"

"No, he's still under the weather." He'd missed almost a week of school already. "Poor thing."

"Then, see? It really is a good thing you've got Ethan around to help you with things."

Piper really, *really* didn't want to talk about Ethan anymore. She nodded at the cinnamon rolls. "Why don't we dig into those? I have a feeling something sweet and gooey will take my mind off waiting to hear about the grant." And other things she would rather forget.

Such as Ethan, whose SUV was crawling up the drive to the sanctuary right this minute. Piper frowned at it through the front window. *Great. Just great.*

So he'd made good on his promise to keep coming back, even after she'd basically kicked him off the property. She wasn't sure whether to be impressed or irritated. She settled on the latter.

Then why have you been peeking out the curtains all morning, wondering if he'd show up?

She may have hated the fact that she'd been on the lookout for him all morning, but one thing was certain—if he'd failed to turn up this time, she wouldn't have called the police. He'd have to fling himself off the mountain right in front of her face before she called Tate Hudson, looking for him again. Even then she still might not do it. Let him crawl back up the mountainside by his fingernails. She wasn't his baby-sitter. Or his wife. It was time to stop acting like she was anything special to him. Because she wasn't. He'd made that perfectly clear. More than once.

You can stop looking at me like that. I'm not one of your wolves, Piper.

And then he was going to leave without saying goodbye. He'd thought it was "for the best." Now he thought it best to stick around and keep trying to stop her from saving homeless wolves. The man was impossible.

She speared a knife through one of the cinnamon rolls with a little too much force. "These look delicious, Zoey. Thank you again."

"My pleasure." Her neighbor turned her head at the sound of Ethan's car door slamming outside. "It seems like you have company."

"Not company." Piper shook her head and kept her gaze glued to the plates and napkins she collected and carried to the table. She'd rather die than have Ethan catch her spying through the window. "Labor. He's only here to get more fodder for that wretched column of his."

"Right. Somehow I doubt that." Zoey grinned as she transferred the cinnamon rolls from their platter to the smaller plates. "Not to be nosy, but…"

Piper picked up one of the rolls, then put it back down. She had a feeling she knew where the conversation was headed, and her appetite had subsequently waned. Significantly. "Don't tell me. You saw the kiss, didn't you?"

Zoey's smile widened. "It was kind of hard not to."

Piper stared down at her plate. She'd hoped that maybe she'd remembered it wrong. That she'd been romanticizing things, and it had been an ordinary, run-of-the-mill kiss. Nothing special. Nothing like the memories that had kept her awake all night.

Apparently she hadn't.

"I have to admit that I was a little surprised," Zoey said. "I mean, we were all kind of under the impression that you two were at each other's throats all the time. I guess the old saying is true."

"What old saying?"

Zoey grinned from ear to ear. "The one about not believing everything you read in the paper."

If Piper ever read another newspaper in her life, it would

be too soon. Was it really so necessary to stay up-to-date on current events? "Oh, you can believe it. Trust me."

"Well, that's not how it looked yesterday. Are you saying that there's not something happening between you two?"

"That's exactly what I'm saying." Her throat closed. Why did she feel like crying all of a sudden?

"So I guess you don't know why he's going to Seattle tomorrow."

"What? Ethan's going to Seattle?" Tomorrow?

Zoey nodded. "Early in the morning. I'm flying him out there on my charter plane. Lucky for him, the group I was supposed to take up to Barrow canceled. Ethan's reservation was just made yesterday morning."

"I see." Yesterday morning? So he'd been planning on not returning to the wolf sanctuary without offering an explanation *and* fleeing the state. Interesting.

Piper stopped short of asking for more information. What Ethan did and where he went was none of her business. Period. At least if he was planning to disappear without a backward glance, she'd been warned this time around.

Someone knocked on the door. Considering she lived on a remote mountainside, her property had been hopping with visitors lately. Too bad none of them were actual paying guests who were interested in the wolves. It seemed she could attract only willful reindeer, their apologetic keepers and journalists with acute cases of wanderlust.

She was pretty certain this most recent caller fell into the last category. "Sorry, Zoey. He probably has a question or something."

"Take your time." Zoey reached for another cinnamon roll.

Piper paused for a deep breath before swinging the door

open. *Do not think about the kiss. Do. Not.* It instantly became the only thing she could think about. *Okay, fine, just don't let him know it's the only thing on your mind. Act like you don't even remember it.*

Hopeless.

"Ethan, hi." She opened the door and focused intently on his neck, not quite trusting herself to meet his gaze or, heaven forbid, accidentally look at his lips.

Unfortunately, like the rest of his physical person, his neck was rather nice. Strong. Manly. *Good grief.* She forced herself to look him in the eye. "This isn't a good time. I have company…"

The protest died on her lips when she took in his grave expression. Something bad had happened. It was written all over his too-handsome face.

"Ethan? What is it?"

"It's Koko." Ethan was near frantic. A caged lion pacing back and forth. "Come quick."

Chapter Twelve

"No." Piper shook her head, clearly not willing to accept that anything could be wrong with her beloved Koko, the favorite of the bunch.

Ethan had worried about this when he'd determined that something wasn't right with the wolf. He knew Piper wouldn't take the news well, especially coming from him. He hadn't wanted to be the one to tell her. He'd hoped he was just being overly cautious when he'd noticed Koko stumbling in his enclosure. But then the wolf had collapsed, and Ethan knew something was wrong. Really wrong.

"I think you need to call someone," he said, as calmly as he could.

But before he got all the words out, Piper ran past him, heading for the wolf enclosures. He started after her, and Zoey quickly caught up with him.

"Ethan, what's going on?" Zoey tripped on a rut in the snow.

He hauled her up by the elbow and kept pressing forward. He could see Piper ahead, already fumbling with the lock on the gate to the pen. "Koko's sick. It doesn't look good."

"I don't understand. Piper said she'd made rounds early

this morning. She didn't mention anything wrong. She even said how frisky and playful Koko seemed."

Ethan shook his head. "I don't know what happened. I just got here, and as soon as I climbed out of my car, I saw him lose his footing. Then he went down."

They reached the enclosure, where Koko lay on the other side of the fence, motionless. Just as he'd been when Ethan had left him. Piper was in a near state of panic, tears falling down her cheeks as she tried to force the gate open.

She dropped her keys, scooped them back up, but couldn't manage to get the proper one in the lock. "I can't." She shook her head and held the keys toward Ethan.

He took them from her trembling hands and released the heavy padlock. "I've got it."

Piper pushed the gate free with a clang and waited for him at the next one, her face pale and her teeth chattering. She'd darted outside without her coat, and the temperature hadn't climbed much since sunup. It still hovered somewhere around the freezing point.

Ethan had an intense urge to wrap his arms around her. For warmth. For comfort.

"Ethan, hurry." Her eyes pleaded with him every bit as much as her words.

"I don't know which key." He held up the ring.

She thumbed through the keys, nearly dropping them twice, and finally landed upon the right one. "Here."

He pushed it into the lock and turned. The second padlock snapped open with a click, and Piper shoved the gate open. She ran to Koko's side and dropped to her knees in the snow. Ethan pocketed the keys and crouched next to her while she rested her hands on the wolf's unconscious body.

"He's breathing." She nodded. A silent sob racked her tiny frame, and she took a deep, shuddering breath.

Ethan could see how hard she was trying to stay composed. He placed his hands next to hers on the animal's broad side. Even in the snow, Koko's coat should have felt warmer than it did. Ethan held his palm to the wolf's nose, expecting to find it cool and wet, as it should have been.

"Dry as a bone," he muttered.

"What's going on? Half an hour ago he was fine." Piper ran her hands over Koko's flank in soothing circles.

Ethan shouted for Zoey, looked up and found her still watching from outside the pen. "Call Stu Foster at the Gold Rush Trail race headquarters. Tell him it's an emergency. And call Tate."

"Will do." She nodded and ran back to the cabin.

"Wh-who's St-Stu Foster?" Piper peered up at him. Her teeth chattered so hard she could barely talk, and her delicate face was beginning to take on a bluish tint.

"You're going to freeze to death out here without a coat. Here." He pulled off his parka and wrapped it around her shoulders, half expecting her to argue with him.

She didn't. She slipped her arms inside and let him zip her all the way in. He tried not to worry about the fact that she was too upset to even argue with him, but she looked so small and uncharacteristically fragile in his oversize parka that he couldn't help it.

"Ethan, who is Stu Foster?" The circular movement of her hands slowed and she balled Koko's pelt in her fists, as if she held on tight enough, maybe he wouldn't slip away. "And why did you ask Zoey to call Tate?"

"Dr. Foster is the lead veterinarian for the Gold Rush Trail sled dog race. He runs a clinic down at race headquarters. He's the most skilled veterinarian in the entire state."

"A specialist? I can't afford that, Ethan." Piper shook her head. "I can barely afford to keep this place running."

No thanks to you.

She didn't say it. She didn't need to. The sentiment hung there in the space between them. Like a thick, impenetrable wall.

"Don't worry about it. I know Stu very well. He flew up to Denali a few times to help out with sick animals in the park. I'll talk to him and see if he'll waive his fee." Ethan was inserting himself deeper and deeper into Piper's world. How long could he keep this up? How long could he straddle the fence like this before he created a mess that he couldn't clean up?

He gazed down at the wolf at his feet. Perhaps now wasn't the time to focus on such an uncomfortable question.

"You'd do that? For one of my wolves?" Piper asked, biting her quivering lower lip. He'd dreamed about her lips last night. Behind her, the sun shimmered white on the snowy landscape. She almost looked as if she was surrounded by spilled diamonds. The visual was such a dazzling, beautiful contrast to what was happening that it made Ethan's chest hurt.

"For you, Piper." He cupped her face in his one of his hands. A lonely tear slipped down her cheek and into his open palm. "I'm doing it for you."

She gave him a bittersweet smile. "Thank you."

Had she thought he would sit there and watch Koko die? He couldn't do that. Not when the animal belonged to Piper. Not now. Maybe not ever.

"I'm not completely heartless, Piper."

"I know." She nodded, but he wasn't quite sure he believed her. "Wait, you never said why you asked Zoey to call Tate. What can he do to help?"

How could Ethan answer that question without alarming

her even more? Especially when he so desperately hoped that he was wrong about the source of Koko's distress.

He looked down at the wolf, resting so still and silent in the snow. Ethan had seen this sort of thing before. In Denali. He'd had the unfortunate experience of seeing it enough times to recognize the warning signs—immediate and severe onset of symptoms, breathing problems, inability to move. If he looked closely, he could see scratches on Koko's muzzle, a sign that the wolf had been pawing at his face, a behavior indicative of pain or a burning sensation in the mouth.

Koko's eyes fluttered open and his paws twitched, as if he was running through an imaginary forest.

Piper bent closer and ran her hand over his head, smoothing back his ears. "Koko? I'm right here, boy. You're doing just fine. You're going to be okay." Her gaze flitted to Ethan. "He's waking up. Surely that's a good sign."

Koko coughed a few times, loud hacking coughs that shook his body from head to tail. He struggled to stand, but his legs folded beneath him and he fell back to his side. His craned his neck, lifted his massive ebony head and blinked a few times. He coughed again, then retched. His stomach churned and he emptied the contents of his stomach onto the snow.

Nausea and vomiting. The only remaining symptoms. It was a textbook case. A chill passed through Ethan that had nothing whatsoever to do with the weather.

"Poor guy. He's got an upset stomach. Maybe that's all it is." Piper looked at him for reassurance, her emerald eyes shining with hope now that Koko had awakened.

Ethan shook his head. "I'm afraid it might be more than that, lovely."

"What aren't you saying?" Her voice broke, and that

little hitch was nearly his undoing. "Ethan, tell me. What is it?"

He hated the words that were about to come out of his mouth. Hated them so much. He would have given anything not to have to say them.

He reached for Piper's hand, still buried in Koko's fur, and covered it with his. Beneath their intertwined fingers, the wolf's wild heartbeat grew weak. *Come on, Koko. Hold on. Hold on, you beast.*

A sound like waves roared in Ethan's ears. *This can't happen. I won't let it.* "Piper, it looks like Koko may have been poisoned."

"Poisoned?" Piper flew to her feet. "No. That can't be possible. It just can't."

She looked around, her gaze darting from the trees to the cluster of rocks in the far corner of the pen. Maybe whoever had done this was still there, hiding behind a tree. Watching. Waiting. But she was too panicked to make herself focus on any one thing.

Nothing made sense anymore. How could this be happening?

Ethan planted his hands on her shoulders and forced her to look him in the eye. His expression was calm, too calm. Beneath his collected exterior, she could see the threat of anger about to overflow. The telltale sign was the sharpening of his gaze. His eyes glittered charcoal-gray. Dark. Deadly.

She shook her head again. "No. No, that can't be it. He can't be poisoned. He's just not feeling well."

But no matter how many times she protested, she couldn't convince herself it was true.

"Piper, listen to me, lovely. We're getting him some help." Ethan was looking at her with the kind of concentration it might take to hold the world together when it was on the verge of falling apart. He'd called her lovely. Only this time, it had actually been sincere.

Which meant this was serious. Gravely serious. The realization hit her with the force of an avalanche—Koko could die.

Her pulse ticked like a bomb in her throat. *No. Please, God. No.* "But who would do something like this? Who?"

Ethan crushed her against his chest and held her so tight that she almost couldn't breathe. Too much was happening. Too much. Too fast. "Help will be here soon."

She wanted so desperately for him to promise that everything would be okay. She needed that reassurance more than she needed oxygen. "Ethan, he's not going to die, is he? Tell me he's not going to die. Promise me."

Lie to me, just this once. Lie to me.

"We're getting him help," he whispered, his voice low and as soft as dandelion puff.

But that wasn't the same thing, was it? It wasn't the same thing at all.

"Tate and Stu Foster are both on their way," Zoey called from the other side of the fence, her fingers curled around the chain link that kept Koko from escaping. From hurting people. So much worry, so much precaution. But things had turned out the other way around, hadn't they? Koko was the one who'd been hurt.

Piper should have seen this coming. The wolves were her pack, and she was their leader. They were her responsibility. She'd made a promise to them and to herself to always protect them. To give them sanctuary.

She'd failed the one and only family she'd ever had.

What was wrong with her? Why couldn't she make things work, even with a pack of wolves? Was it really such a bad thing to want a family? To want someone to love, and to be loved in return?

She took a deep breath and smiled through the tears she could no longer keep from falling. "Thank you, Zoey."

"Piper, they'll be here any minute. I promise." Zoey stood no less than fifteen feet away, but somehow that space felt impossibly large. A cavernous gulf. Everything seemed different. Distorted. The morning sun moved behind the clouds, and the sky, swollen with snow, felt as if it was pressing down on Piper. She couldn't breathe. She couldn't get enough air.

Because for the first time, the wild, beautiful world she had created for herself—the only world where she felt safe enough to live and love—felt as if it might be nothing but an illusion.

"Describe to me again exactly what you saw when you first arrived on the property this morning." Tate scanned the contents of his police notepad and looked expectantly at Ethan. He'd been jotting things down all day, and it was beginning to grate on Ethan's nerves.

He wanted action. He needed Tate to do something.

"Do we really have to go over this again?" He felt like jumping out of his skin. How long did Tate expect him to stand here on the opposite side of the fence while Piper was in there beside Stu Foster? They were bent over Koko, who'd managed to wake up before help arrived. But the wolf's copper eyes were cloudy and distant. He didn't seem capable of focusing on any one thing. Not even Piper.

On a normal day, she was his sun. The center of his orbit. That wolf never took his eyes off her.

"Look, I know you want to get back in there. I know Piper needs you right now," Tate said.

Ethan glanced at Piper. Did she need him? Really? He

wasn't even sure. But he knew one thing—he needed to be beside her.

"I'm just doing my job," Tate added. "You want me to get to the bottom of this, don't you?"

"Yes. Yes, of course." Ethan lowered his voice. "But you and I both know who did this."

"Who?" Tate asked blithely. His composure was beginning to grate on Ethan's nerves.

He knew Tate was simply doing his job, being a professional. But it was hard to understand how anyone could be so calm, when Ethan himself felt as if there was a wild animal inside him, trying to claw its way out.

Get ahold of yourself. Losing your mind isn't going to help anyone, least of all Piper. "The person who left the graffiti is the same person who poisoned the wolf. It's rather obvious, isn't it?"

"No. Not obvious." Tate shook his head. "For starters, we don't even know for sure that the wolf was poisoned."

He couldn't be serious. Had they not just witnessed Stu Foster administering activated charcoal to Koko so all the toxins could be purged from his system? "The animal was poisoned, Tate. Without a doubt."

"We'll see. Stu is taking three vials of blood for testing. We won't have the toxicology report back until tomorrow morning. Maybe even tomorrow afternoon."

Ethan's fists involuntary clenched at his sides. He felt like punching someone.

Tate sighed. "Look, I know this is frustrating. But we can't make assumptions. Investigations don't work that way, and I want to get to the bottom of this as much as you do. Got it?"

On a purely cerebral level, Ethan understood what his friend was saying. He even agreed with it. But every time he thought about the faraway, wounded look in Piper's eyes when he'd told her that he'd suspected Koko had been poisoned, all rational thinking flew right out the window. "Got it."

"So once again, describe everything that you saw."

Ethan's gaze flitted back toward the pen, where Stu was setting up an IV for the wolf. Piper looked shell-shocked, smaller and more vulnerable than he would have ever imagined, still wearing his oversize parka. Someone should get her a blanket. And some mittens. Maybe even a sleeping bag. He knew there'd be no dragging her from the enclosure until Koko was out of the woods. If that didn't happen, if things ended as badly as Ethan thought they might...

He couldn't even imagine how she'd react if Koko didn't survive. He remembered with heartbreaking clarity what had happened when the alpha female of one of the oldest wolf packs in Denali had been shot by a hunter. For eight straight nights, the canyon echoed with the mournful howls of her pack. They'd stood by her, even in death. *We are here. We are here and we remember you.*

The other wolves, five in all, had remained loyally by her fallen carcass and refused to move. The hunter hadn't even been able to collect his kill, fearful for his life. At last they'd moved on, but without the fallen wolf's mate, the alpha male. He'd buried himself in the snowy hillside, so still that Ethan had mistaken him for a downed log. He'd abdicated his role as alpha and abandoned his pack. He'd become a rarity, a lone wolf. A beaten and broken prizefighter.

There was a reason why lone wolves were an uncommon sight. They didn't last long. Wolves needed their pack to survive. Ethan hadn't been at all surprised when he'd arrived in the canyon one morning to find the wolf gone. All that was left of him was a trail of crimson blood in the snow. There'd been no other wolves to mourn his loss, no aching, desolate howls cast to the sky. But Ethan had somehow felt those howls rattling around in his rib cage. A nighttime elegy.

He felt them now, again, when he looked at Piper.

He cleared his throat and directed his focus once again on Tate. "I told you. I was only here for a few minutes when I noticed that the wolf seemed out of sorts. Everything happened very quickly."

"You didn't notice any suspicious vehicles or people?" Tate double-checked his notes.

"No." For the thousandth time. "Just like before, on the day of the graffiti. Except this time, Zoey's car was in the driveway alongside Piper's. Other than that, nothing."

"No one left the area after you'd arrived? Perhaps while you were inside talking to Piper?"

"I didn't go inside. I got straight to work." Ethan shifted his weight from one foot to the other. "Piper and I aren't exactly on friendly terms. Or we weren't. I'm not even sure anymore."

Tate lifted a sardonic brow. "So you really took our talk this morning to heart, I see?"

"Tate." Ethan's voice sounded lethal even to himself.

"Sorry. We're all tense, okay?" He flipped his notebook closed. "I'm going to take a look around, maybe shoot some photos. Zoey called Posy, and the recital committee is on their way over with food. She figured cooking is the last thing on Piper's mind at the moment."

Ethan couldn't see Piper having much of an appetite, but it was nice to see the community rallying around her. It would do her good to spend more time with people. "So I'm free to go now?"

Tate pocketed his notebook and pulled out his camera phone. "Is that what you want to do? Leave?"

No. Not at all.

He wanted to stand beside Piper. He wanted to tell her that she could lean on him. She didn't need to be strong on her own anymore. She didn't need to be a lone wolf.

But it was turning into Grand Central Station around here. Liam Blake had already shown up with a half dozen kids from the youth group, and they were finishing the chores. The dance recital crew would be here any minute with food. Did Piper even want him around?

He wholeheartedly doubted it.

She'd reached for him in those first few minutes, before half the town had descended. She'd clung to him as if he were a shelter in a storm. But what about now?

He glanced at his cell phone to check the time. In less than twenty-four hours he was scheduled to arrive in Seattle. His flight to Anchorage on Zoey's charter plane left at six in the morning.

He inhaled a ragged breath and answered Tate's question. "I'm going to stick around. At least for a little while."

"Good." Tate's gaze flitted to the tree-lined drive, where yet another car had arrived. A man Ethan didn't recognize climbed out of the driver's side, glanced around and walked toward the cabin. "Who's that?"

Ethan frowned. "I don't know, but I'm about to find out."

"You and me both," Tate said.

Ethan cast a final glance in the direction of Koko's enclosure before heading for the cabin alongside Tate. Piper seemed far too busy assisting Stu with the IV to notice anything beyond the fence.

By the time the two men reached the steps of the cabin, the stranger had already knocked on the door and was trying to peer in the front window.

Ethan tapped on his shoulder. "Can I help you?"

"Do you work here?" The man turned around, casting a sideways glance at the state trooper badge pinned to Tate's chest.

Ethan cleared his throat. "In a way."

"My name is Jack Oliver." He offered his hand for a shake. A brown leather briefcase dangled from the opposite hand, a sure sign he was an out-of-towner. Ethan had never seen a briefcase within Aurora city limits. He wasn't sure he'd ever seen one anywhere in Alaska, for that matter. "I just flew in yesterday from Washington, DC."

"DC? Really?" Tate said. "What brings you to Alaska?"

But Ethan already knew.

Jack Oliver had to be the businessman that Zoey had picked up from Juneau. *Some government official...*

Now? *Really, God?* Ethan knew he had no right to question God's timing. He'd only recently begun praying again. But didn't Piper have enough on her plate at the moment?

Jack Oliver smiled. Poor guy. He had no idea what kind of mess he'd traveled all this way to see. "I'm with the National Nature Conservatory. This facility has applied for a government grant, and I'm here to conduct an inspection. May I speak to Piper Quinn? She's the director of the facility, is she not?"

"I'm afraid she's indisposed at the moment." Ethan hated the fact that he'd been right. Why couldn't this guy have been a traveling salesman or something?

The irony of the situation wasn't lost on Ethan. He'd been against the NNC funding since day one. He'd sat by and watched Piper struggle with the paperwork, and he hadn't once offered to help, despite the fact that he'd applied for six such grants himself in Denali. All of which had been successfully awarded.

But this wasn't how things should have gone down. He didn't want to win this way. This wasn't a fair fight. Piper didn't stand a chance. Passing the inspection didn't seem possible when the sanctuary had basically become a crime scene, and the star wolf was busy fighting for his life.

"She's indisposed?" Jack Oliver let out a laugh that sounded far too haughty for Ethan's taste. "Sir, perhaps you're not aware, but agency rules stipulate the premises must be made available for inspection in order for the grant application to move forward. We were very impressed by Ms. Quinn's documentation of her work with wolves, but this sanctuary can't be approved for funding without an inspection."

"An inspection isn't possible right now." Ethan stepped between Jack Oliver and the enclosures. The last thing the man needed to see was a semiconscious wolf hooked up to an IV, although it was probably clear from all the activity that something was amiss.

And why exactly do you think it's your place to protect these wolves?

It wasn't about the wolves. It was about Piper, and not letting her get kicked while she was already down. Ethan would have done the same for anyone. His actions didn't have a thing to do with the wolves themselves. Or love.

Love.

Where had that thought come from? The stress of the situation was getting to him. He'd been thinking about Tate's romantic notions that he and Piper somehow belonged together. Which was nonsense. Obviously.

"Again, I'm sorry," he said in a low voice. "Perhaps another time. Because I'm actually up to speed on NNC rules, and I believe there are provisions for an amended application in certain situations."

Jack Oliver deflated. Slightly. "In rare cases, yes. But it's most uncommon. Amendments to applications are permitted once, and then only when the facility has undergone significant changes in personnel or quality of care."

"Just as I said. Uncommon." Ethan smiled. "But not impossible."

"No, not impossible." The inspector glanced at his watch—a fancy-looking silver thing, another clear indication that he wasn't from around here. "I'll be on my way, then. I have another facility to visit before I head back to Washington in the morning. I trust you'll tell Ms. Quinn I was here."

"Oh, I will." When the time was right, not when she was standing vigil over Koko like that mournful lone wolf.

Ethan tried to shake that tragic visual from his consciousness while Jack Oliver got back in his car and drove away. He failed. That sad wolf, nothing more than a ghost of what he'd once been, had made his home in Ethan's head.

He remembered long, bitter nights digging snow caves under the dim glow of a headlight strapped around his skull. For ten consecutive nights after the lone wolf had gone missing, Ethan had wandered the camp trying to find him. He dug caves, makeshift dens, in the unlikely event that the wolf was still alive and needed a place to rest and recuperate. On the tenth night, a blizzard had blown in off Bristol Bay, and Ethan had suffered pretty severe frostbite. He'd nearly lost a finger, all because of those snow caves. It had been a waste of his time in the end. He never found the wolf.

He squeezed his eyes shut, trying to force the sad creature back into the forest of memory. When he opened them, he found Tate watching him with a sad smile.

"That was a good thing you just did," he said, nodding toward Jack Oliver's car rolling back toward the highway. "And you keep insisting you don't belong here."

Why couldn't Ethan shake the tragic recollection of that lone wolf? Probably because he hadn't been able to save him. And he couldn't seem to save Piper, either.

He wouldn't. Not in the long run. Too many words had been written. Too much damage had been done.

"Trust me. I don't."

Chapter Thirteen

Piper's brain hurt.

She wasn't technically sure that was possible in a biological sense, but hers did. She was sure of it. For hours now, she'd been concentrating so hard on every word that came out of Dr. Stu Foster's mouth, but there'd been so many of them. Frightening words. Words she didn't want to have to wrap her mind around. Words like *ventricular arrhythmia* and *cardiogenic shock*. And worst of all— *mortality rate*.

"It looks like the charcoal treatment worked. The first one cleared him of gastric content. I performed a second treatment as a precaution, and nothing came back up." Stu removed his stethoscope from around his neck, inserted the earpieces and pressed the chest piece against the matted fur on Koko's side.

She knew it had to be her imagination, but the animal seemed so much thinner already. In the course of a day, her big black wolf had been transformed into a bag of bones. Plus he was filthy from the charcoal treatments and their ensuing sickness. She could barely tolerate looking at him like this. She wanted to give him a bath and brush his hair, which had to be one of the most nonsensical thoughts she'd ever had.

And she was tired. So very tired. She wished she could close her eyes, fall asleep and wake up when this nightmare had ended.

"His breathing is still much shallower than I'd like." Stu moved the stethoscope around a few more times and listened intently, his face a mask of concentration.

Piper bit the inside of her cheek to keep herself from crying, because she knew once she started, she might not ever stop.

"We've done all that we can do for now." The vet pulled the stethoscope out of his ears and let it hang around his neck again. A lifesaver's necklace. Or so she hoped. "I've put a heavy dose of electrolytes in his IV, along with some nutrients, to replace the fluids that he's lost. I'm also giving him a sedative to keep him calm so he can sleep off the effects of the poison."

The hard knot that had lodged in Piper's throat hours ago tripled in size. She couldn't seem to swallow. Or breathe. "So you do think that's what it is? Poison?"

Her knees buckled. She needed to sit down again before she collapsed. She sank into the snow. It seeped through her jeans with prickly cold wetness, which she barely noticed. Her discomfort didn't matter, anyway. Nothing mattered.

Someone had tried to kill one of her wolves.

How could she go on after this? Even if Koko survived—and right now, survival hardly seemed a given—how could she stay in a place where her wolves were so despised that someone had done this?

It was over. Her sanctuary. Her dream. All of it.

Stu crouched down in the snow beside her and placed a reassuring hand on her knee. "Yes, Piper. I'm afraid that's what it looks like. Koko's symptoms are indicative of acute poisoning. We won't know for certain until the toxicology reports come back."

"I see." She nodded absently. His voice sounded faraway and strange, as if he was speaking to her from the bottom of a well. She wondered if she might be going into shock. Probably. Wasn't that what happened when people lost a loved one?

"Try not to take this so hard. Koko's not out of the woods, but he's still with us. He might pull out of it. Right now all we can do is wait." Stu placed a hand on her knee in a gesture she was sure was meant to comfort her. But she didn't feel it. She couldn't feel a thing anymore. The cold. The wind. Nothing.

She swallowed. Or tried, anyway. The lump in her throat refused to budge, and she coughed instead. "Wh-where? Where do we wait? At the hospital?"

Koko would hate that. When he woke up—*if* he woke up—the bright florescent lights and all the strange smells would bring back so many terrible memories. Memories that had taken Piper years to help him overcome.

Stu shook his head. "I could take him to the clinic, but I don't think that's a good idea. Most wolves do best in their own environment. I'm afraid to place him under any more stress than he's already encountered. I think it's best that he stay right here where he's comfortable. This is his home."

This is his home. For how much longer? This land, Alaska, everything she'd ever dreamed of—she felt as if it was all slipping through her fingers.

"Good." She nodded and somehow did a passable impression of someone who wasn't on the verge of falling apart.

"Is there anyone I can call for you, Piper? You seem… well, distraught. That's a completely normal, understandable reaction. I just don't think you should try to deal with this alone."

Okay, so maybe her facade wasn't believable, after all.

"There's no one." Never had those words cut so close to the bone. "I mean, I'm not alone. See?" She waved a hand toward the surrounding acreage.

Stu chuckled under his breath. "You have a point. Half the town is in your front yard. Aurora does a good job of taking care of its own. I just wondered if there was anyone special you wanted by your side."

She looked up. Sure enough, people were milling about everywhere. She'd been so focused on what was going on inside Koko's enclosure that she'd forgotten the world beyond the chain-link fence even existed. When she'd gestured to the rest of the sanctuary and said she wasn't alone, she'd been talking about the others. The wolves—Tundra, Shasta, Echo, Whisper and Fury. She hadn't meant actual people.

Only now, after seeing Stu point to all the folks on the other side of the fence, did she realize how profoundly sad such a mistake seemed.

"I hate to say this, but you're going to need to keep an eye on him tonight. In the event that he wakes up, we don't want him pulling that IV out of his leg." Stu ran his hands along the shaved spot on Koko's right foreleg where he'd inserted a catheter. "It looks good and secure right now, and we want it to stay that way."

"Absolutely. I won't leave his side." She would have stayed, even if Stu had ordered her gone. Leaving Koko alone right now was inconceivable. "Um, Stu, I have a question."

He looked up from his vet bag, where he'd almost finished storing away all the supplies he'd used over the course of the morning and afternoon. "Yes."

"What if Koko doesn't wake up?" It hurt to ask the question aloud. Her throat burned from the effort it took to articulate her worst fear. "I mean, is it possible that he won't?"

Stu's gaze dropped to Koko, sleeping peacefully in the snow. And she knew. Before he even said it, she knew.

He looked back up and leveled his gaze at her. "I'm going to be honest, Piper. Koko is really sick. I wish I knew what kind of toxin he'd ingested. That kind of knowledge is crucial. It would help me make decisions regarding his treatment. But since we don't know, I'm administering the broadest possible range of treatment protocols. At this point, based on what little we know, I'd say he's got a fifty-fifty chance of making it through the night."

Fifty-fifty. Like two sides of a coin. How did that old childhood saying go? *Heads, I win. Tails, you lose.* What she would do for a two-headed nickel right now.

Fifty-fifty. Please, God. Don't let him die.

She lifted her eyes to the sky, where twilight dripped gray overhead. Moody, like a bruise. Like the storm clouds she'd seen in Ethan's eyes right before he'd kissed her.

"Stu, actually, there is someone I'd like you to get for me. If he's still here, that is." What was she doing? Ethan wasn't her boyfriend. He wasn't even technically a friend. But right now, he was the one she wanted. The only one. His parka was still wrapped around her, enveloping her in the comfort of his smoky pine scent. Like a fireside embrace. She needed more. She needed to feel his arms around her again. Only for tonight. Just one more time.

Besides, what else could possibly go wrong? The worst had already happened. Hadn't it?

"Could you find Ethan for me?"

Ethan narrowed his gaze at the vet. "Me? Are you sure?"

Stu nodded. He looked exactly like one might expect a person to look after he'd spent a day trying to save an animal from a mysterious poisoning. Exhausted. "Yes. She's pretty shaken up. These animals obviously mean a great deal to her. I'm not sure she should be alone tonight. The next eight hours are crucial for Koko. Honestly, it could go either way."

"Right." Ethan nodded. He'd hoped for better news.

"I asked her if there was anyone special she wanted by her side, and she asked for you." Stu glanced in the direction of Koko's enclosure, where Piper sat in the snow with the wolf's head in her lap.

Ethan knew that if he left and returned the next morning, he'd find her in that exact same spot. If losing Koko was a real possibility—and Stu certainly seemed to think it was—she wouldn't leave the wolf's side. The thought of her keeping vigil all alone made his gut ache.

She'd asked for him, of all people. If that didn't put an exclamation mark on just how alone she was, nothing would. He shouldn't be the one she wanted. Given everything that had happened in the past ten days, she should have asked for anyone but him.

But she hadn't. Had she?

"Well?" Stu looked at him, waiting for an answer.

Ethan had every reason to say no. His column, for one. He was due to turn it in at midnight. In light of the day's events, he had plenty to write about. Of his entire series on the wolf sanctuary, this would likely be the pivotal piece. A story about a wolf's life hanging in the balance after being poisoned? Readers would eat it up.

And then there was his interview in Seattle. His flight out of Aurora was at sunup. Seattle was his future. Alaska wasn't. Piper wasn't.

Anyone in his position would say no.

He nodded. "Okay, then."

He'd miss his deadline. An unpardonable offense, especially for a reporter who was already skating on thin ice with his editor. Lou was sure to fire him, if not outright strangle him. With any luck, Ethan would manage to land the job in Seattle. He could still catch his flight. He had to. It was either that, face unemployment or embark on a new career in hotel management.

Stu gave him a grim smile. "You've got my number. You two call me if anything changes."

"Will do," Ethan said, and watched Stu's truck make the long crawl down Piper's snowy drive.

He gathered a few things from his SUV—thermal blanket, battery-operated lantern, hand warmer packets. Sleeping in his car those few nights when he was keeping an eye out on the sanctuary had proved at least a little helpful. He may have failed to keep Piper's wolves safe, but he could keep her warm for a night.

"Hi." She looked up when he pushed open the gate to Koko's pen. Her smile was bittersweet and uncharacteristically bashful.

"Hi." He felt as if he was on a first date, which was a preposterous thing to think in light of the circumstances.

"Thank you." Her gaze flitted to the lifeless wolf sprawled across her lap, then back to him. "For staying, I mean."

"Of course." He wedged the lantern into the snow and flipped it on.

Piper's face glowed gold and ethereal in its dim light. "I hope I'm not keeping you from anything."

Ethan settled down beside her and wrapped the thermal blanket around both of them. It was barely large enough for two. Sitting so close to Piper immediately sent waves of awareness crashing over him. He inhaled a steadying breath and caught the scent of flowers from her hair. Poppies and hollyhocks. Alaskan blooms.

He swallowed and felt as if he was swallowing glass. This was going to be a long night. "No, nothing special. You save me from a boring night in front of the television."

If she didn't believe him, she gave no indication. He kept his gaze glued to Koko, though, just in case.

She cleared her throat. "It was awfully nice of so many people to stop by today."

Ethan nodded. Were they going to make small talk all night? It didn't seem right. The church folks, the women from the recital committee and the youth group had all gone home by now. Darkness had fallen. Darkness so thick it felt as if the whole world was asleep. Tonight wasn't a night for chitchat. Maybe it was the way the snow glimmered like sugar under the starlight. Maybe it was the closeness of Piper's thigh pressing against his. Maybe it was the way Koko's breathing sounded far too slow and labored. Whatever the reason, the night deserved more than small talk.

Ethan wanted to know her. Really know her. Maybe it was the reporter in him, but he needed to understand how she'd ended up here. She'd told him bits and pieces, but he still didn't know how things began. Why wolves? "Tell me something. How did you get started with all this?"

"You mean the wolves?" She smiled again, and this time there was the barest hint of joy in her eyes. "Are you asking me how I started rescuing them?"

"Yes." It was a question that had haunted him since the moment he'd first laid eyes on her, but for some reason he'd been either unable or unwilling to ask. Maybe because a part of him dreaded hearing the answer. "Tell me about the first wolf."

"Okay." She stroked Koko's head, pausing. Remembering. "I was sixteen. For days, a stray dog had been hanging around an abandoned building that I passed every day when I walked to school. At least I thought it was a dog."

"It was a wolf?"

"No." She shook her head. "A hybrid."

Hybrids, animals that resulted from the pairing of a wolf with a domestic dog, were extremely rare in nature. Humans bred them, sometimes with the intention to create a "perfect" watchdog, and other times, simply because they could. Whatever the reason, it was typically a mistake. Hybrids made challenging pets, often too territorial to blend into a normal household. Because even a little bit wild is still wild. "Ah."

"I didn't know it at the time, of course. I didn't know anything about wolves at all back then. All I knew was that every day when I passed that building, I saw an animal that was obviously hungry. And obviously homeless." Her voice lowered to barely above a whisper, as if she were imparting a secret. Something she didn't want to tell the mountain or the trees. Not even the wolves. Only Ethan. "I guess I identified with that animal. I was in my sixth foster home, and I wasn't any more wanted there than I had been at the others."

He took her hand. Her fingers, cold as ice, wrapped around his and squeezed. Tight. As if she was in danger of drifting away if she didn't hold on to him.

"I started saving food. Bits and pieces of leftover dinner. Sometimes I skipped my meals altogether so I could bring that dog something to eat. I gained his trust that way. After a couple weeks, he let me put a rope around his neck and I took him home."

Ethan had a few guesses where this story was going, and none of the possible scenarios playing out in his head were good. "What happened next?"

"My foster parents were furious, of course. They said

they could barely afford to feed me, much less an enormous, flea-bitten stray. I was devastated. I begged. I cried. I even considered running away. Finally, I settled on taking the dog to the local animal shelter. At least that way, they could find the poor thing a permanent home. A real family."

"So I took the dog to the shelter, and the staff promised me I could stop by for visits until he was adopted. I left in tears, but knew that deep down I was doing the right thing. I'd done all that I could do. I let myself think that the dog would get adopted, find a forever home and live happily ever after. When I went to the shelter after school the next day, and the dog's cage was empty, I thought that's what had happened."

Ethan closed his eyes, not wanting to hear the rest. He knew it had been something like this. Some painful genesis that could never be undone. Something he couldn't fix.

He opened his eyes, and she shook her head. "The shelter vet had identified the dog as a wolf hybrid and immediately euthanized him. They said he was too dangerous to place in a home. I knew better. I'd fed that animal by hand for nearly two weeks. I'd bathed him with a garden hose in the front yard of the house where I lived. He'd licked my face and let me hug him. I couldn't remember the last time I'd hugged someone like that. But that animal, that wolf they thought was so deadly, had let me."

Ethan's arms ached to hold her. It took every ounce of self-restraint he possessed not to reach for her. *The house where I'd lived.* Not her home. *My foster parents.* Not her family.

The differences weren't lost on him.

All this time, she'd been trying to create a family for herself. A place where she belonged. In rescuing those animals, she'd rescued herself. And along Ethan had come and systematically, day by day, word by word, torn what was left of her world apart.

"So that's the story of the first wolf. He's the only one I lost, the only one I failed." A single tear slid down her cheek. "Until now."

"Don't," Ethan said, more firmly than he intended. "Don't think like that. There's still time." It was running out, though. Each second, each minute, each hour that Koko didn't wake up brought them closer to the end.

"I know. It's just…" Her gaze fixed on something behind him, and she smiled and pointed to the sky. "Look."

Ethan turned to see a wisp of color dancing in the northern sky. Pale pink. "The auroras."

The northern lights were back, just like the night he'd told her about the bear attack. And once again, Ethan was tempted to believe in signs. Not folk tales like the *revontulet* fox fires. But reminders of a real and caring God. If those pink lights stood for something, if they were more than just a scientific phenomenon, he would have liked to think they meant God was there. He knew the secret hurts they'd both carried for so long. Releasing those burdens meant something. Something so profound it had to be written across the sky.

He was going to kiss her again. Piper could feel it coming this time.

The moment Ethan saw the auroras, his expression changed. And when he turned back around, he looked at her with eyes filled with awe and wonder. As if he'd seen something exquisite for the first time in his life, a rare orchid or a delicate bird that had been thought to be long extinct. But he wasn't looking at a flower or a bird. Nor was he looking at the auroras. He was looking directly at her.

"I'm sorry, lovely," he whispered, and brought his hand to her face. "About everything."

I'm sorry.

Words she'd never heard from her mother. Once upon a time, when she was a little girl, she'd thought those words could fix things. If her mother had ever come for her, they would have. *Baby girl, I'm sorry.* That's all it would have taken. Piper would have followed her anywhere and forgiven all.

Things had changed by the time Stephen had come into her life. Or maybe it was just that she herself had changed. She'd grown up. She'd made a life for herself. She knew she didn't need anyone. Not people, anyway. She'd survived her entire adulthood with no one but the wolves, and it had been okay. Maybe not perfect, but okay. An apology didn't carry the same weight it once had. Not that Stephen had ever come right out and apologized.

I'm sorry, lovely. About everything.

They were just words. But right here, right now, with a dying wolf in her lap and the auroras dancing overhead, Ethan couldn't have said anything more perfect.

His hands slid through her hair until he cradled her face. Piper could see a world of color in his eyes, and though she knew it was only the auroras reflected back at her, it seemed like more, like an apology for every wrong she'd ever experienced. And his touch carried the promise of a balm.

She swallowed hard. The sky glowed pink and violet, the colors of romance and lilacs and the rebirth of spring. Snow fell around them like falling stars. And with excruciating slowness, Ethan's gaze dropped to her mouth.

He was definitely going to kiss her again. But only if she didn't kiss him first.

She leaned into him, and their lips met. Two long-lost travelers who'd finally found their way home.

Piper was suddenly spent, more exhausted than she'd ever felt in her life. She felt as if the weight of her past and that of every wolf she cared for was pressing down on her. So much time. So much pain. She wasn't sure she could do it anymore. Not by herself.

She kissed Ethan as if it was the last breath she'd ever take, as if she was gasping for air. He stroked her hair, whispered words of comfort and told her everything was going to be fine. Koko would wake up. The sanctuary would survive. She would be okay. And in that moment, she loved Ethan for it. She'd never heard such beautiful lies.

"Sleep, lovely. I'm here. You're not alone. Not this time." He pressed a kiss to her hair, and she dropped her head to his shoulder and burrowed into the crook of his neck. To that warm, intimate place where his pine scent and beautiful words lived. And that smell, that warmth, those lovely sentiments she wanted so desperately to believe, they were all as soothing as a lullaby.

Ethan held Piper as she drifted off to sleep, his mind fixed on the idea of memories and how they shaped people. How they'd shaped Piper. How they'd shaped him.

How strangely sad it was that some experiences burned themselves into one's being like a forest fire, destroying everything in its path—relationships, hopes, dreams and faith. Moments and lifetimes lost. Until by some act of godly grace, something happened to break the stifling hold of those traumatic memories. Feelings long forgotten were brought back to the forefront, at times in the blinding light of an amethyst sky, and other times, in the quiet hush of snow falling on a wolf's dark pelt.

Ethan had known something was happening to him from the first day he stepped onto Piper's land. He'd fought it. He'd fought it as best he could. But how long could a person fight something as exquisite as sanctuary?

It still didn't seem quite real—the idea that he could finally be free. He knew it with his head, and he knew it with his ears, as he listened to the mournful howl of the wolves, their saddest of songs in the bitter Alaskan night. But for all Ethan's newly recovered awareness, he still didn't know it in his heart. It was almost as if the bear attack had altered him to such an extent that he couldn't possibly be the same man who'd carried a dying coyote along the banks of the Last Fork River or had dug snow caves until his hands bled. All for a wolf. Where had that man gone?

He wanted to be that man again, at long last. For Piper. For Koko. For himself.

He reached out and rested his hands on Koko's back. It was the first time he'd touched a wolf since he'd come back to volunteer at the sanctuary. All this time, he'd steadfastly avoided actual physical contact. As if he'd known a touch was all it would take. As if things could be so simple.

Maybe they could. It felt that way now. At long last.

He held on for dear life—for his life, for Piper's, for Koko's. He buried his hands in the wolf's ebony fur and wept like a baby. Reborn.

He wasn't sure how long the three of them stayed that way. Him. Piper. Koko. Together under the stars. Long enough for the indigo darkness to fade to a sparkling sapphire blue. Long enough for Piper to stir and awaken. But not long enough to see any change in Koko.

"He's still asleep," she whispered, and the grief in her voice almost broke Ethan's heart all over again.

"But he's still alive," Ethan said. "I think we should call Stu. Maybe there's something he can do."

"Okay." She nodded. "But my phone is in the cabin."

"Mine's in the car. I'll get yours, and I'll bring you something warm to drink. I'll be right back. I promise." He pressed a kiss to her forehead.

He hated to leave her, even for a second, but he wanted Stu here. Ethan couldn't keep sitting around, waiting for the wolf to die. And he *really* couldn't stand watching Piper do the same.

When he let himself into the cabin, a shaft of pink light from the auroras drifted through the narrow opening in the curtains, illuminating a vase of flowers in the center of the rustic pine table that Piper apparently used as both her dining table and makeshift desk. Books on ecology, animal husbandry and wildlife management were stacked five deep. A pile of papers had been placed neatly on top of her closed MacBook computer. Ethan recognized the seal at the top of one of the pages as the insignia for the National Nature Conservancy.

Her grant paperwork.

He had a mind to take a look at it and see if there were any adjustments or additions he could make in order to improve her chances for an amended application. But now wasn't the time. He needed to get back outside and check on Piper. He was worried about her. Koko still hadn't regained consciousness, and already the auroras were growing fainter and fainter, like a faded watercolor painting. Dawn loomed upon them with all its fatal implications.

Time was running out.

He strode toward the door, but something made him pause. He couldn't put his finger on what it was. A feeling. An impression of something out of place.

He turned back around and took in the cozy scene with

Piper's books and papers, pieces of her life he wanted to thumb through so he could know her better. The tiny room glowed pink as a cherry blossom. Ethan felt as if he was looking at it through rose-colored glasses. Then, as the auroras ebbed and flowed, the hue faded to a whisper of blush. Ethan blinked. Everything looked different all of a sudden, most notably the flowers in the center of the table.

Only now did he notice the ultraviolet petals, so bright they almost looked blue. Soft velvet trumpets, all clustered together and dangling elegantly from their shooting green stems like a blooming chandelier.

Ethan couldn't believe what he was seeing. He took a step closer, just to be sure, and bent to inspect the lush bouquet, careful not to touch them with his bare hands. As he did, Piper's voice resonated in his soul, as real as if she were whispering in his ear.

Open his eyes, Lord.

He blinked, and knew with absolute certainty what he was looking at—the key to the mystery. The answer.

Those flowers. They were a special variety, one that thrived in melting snow. Alpine aconite, sometimes called by their more common name, wolfsbane.

Queen of the poisons.

Chapter Fourteen

While Ethan was gone, Piper rested her head on Koko's still form—face-to-face, her skin against the velvety softness of his thick, dark fur.

"Wake up. Please wake up," she whispered, her breath sending waves rippling through his ebony pelt.

This couldn't be the end. It didn't feel right. All through the night, while she'd been talking to Ethan, she'd been trying to prepare herself for this. For goodbye. Beneath the beauty of the night, amid the auroras, the swirling skies and even the wonder of Ethan's kiss, the ending had loomed. The culmination of everything she'd ever wanted. Dreams dashed.

And now that the enchanting pink sky grew dim and faded before her eyes, she could no longer pretend it wasn't coming. The breaking dawn.

Still, it didn't seem real. She squeezed her eyes closed and rested her palms on Koko's side.

Open his eyes, Lord.

"Piper!"

She jerked upright and saw Ethan coming toward her through the snow in a blizzard of euphoria. He screamed her name again, too loud for the quiet hour. He seemed almost triumphant, which made no sense at all.

"Piper!"

"What's wrong?" she asked, fingertips buried in Koko's fur. She couldn't let go. Not now. Not yet. She knew it was almost time, but she just couldn't.

He flew through the double gates, carrying something in his hands. Flowers. Dazzling purple blossoms. At first Piper simply thought it odd that he would choose such an unlikely moment to give her a bouquet. Where had he gotten them, anyway?

Then she recognized them as the ones Caleb had given her. "What are you doing with those?"

He'd wrapped the stems in a plastic bag and held them away from his body, arm extended as far as humanly possible. "Where did you get these?"

"Caleb gave them to me."

"Where?" he demanded. "Where did Caleb get them?"

"He picked them for me. Right here on the grounds. I'm not sure where, exactly," she said, but Ethan only seemed to be half listening. His gaze scanned the horizon, flitting frantically from one end of the enclosure to the other. "Ethan, why are you acting like this? You're scaring me."

"The flowers are what made Koko sick, Piper. They're poisonous."

She wanted to argue with him. They couldn't possibly be poisonous. They couldn't. Because if they were, then she was the one who'd made Koko sick. She'd penned him in an enclosure with poisonous plants.

But she could tell by the dire look on Ethan's face that he was certain. She swallowed. *What have I done?* "Poisonous? Are you sure?"

"Quite sure. The plant is called Alpine aconite, but its nickname is wolfsbane, because it was once used to…"

"Kill wolves." Her fists balled in Koko's fur.

Oh my goodness.

Piper had heard about wolfsbane. The ancient Greeks had used it to poison arrows when hunting wolves. In more recent centuries, farmers had poisoned meat with it and left the tainted food out at night for wolves that threatened their livestock. She'd read about wolfsbane in books, articles and online. And never once had she imagined that it was growing on her property. Right here. In Koko's pen.

She tried to take comfort in the fact that the flowers weren't growing in any of the other pens, and that Caleb had been picking the blooms. Otherwise Koko could have eaten even more of them. But right here, right now, with Koko as sick as he was, it was difficult to look on the bright side.

Piper grew very still.

Caleb's been picking the flowers.

"Wait," she said. "Isn't it possible for the toxins in wolfsbane to be absorbed through the skin?"

"Yes, which is precisely why I'm not touching the stems."

Piper felt the blood drain from her face. She thought she might faint. "Caleb. He's been sick for a week. He picked those flowers with his bare hands and even put them in a vase for me."

"We need to call Stu Foster. And we need to call Tate," Ethan said. "Right now."

He pressed her cell phone into her hand, and she shook so badly that she could barely dial. Within twenty minutes Tate arrived, with Stu sitting beside him in the front seat of his squad car. It had been such a long, quiet night, and now everything seemed to be happening at warp speed.

Even the wolves seemed to sense the urgency of the situation. They paced back and forth in their enclosures, yipping and pawing at the fence. Even Tundra, the shyest of the bunch, had come out from behind the aspens and sat sentry at the fence line.

"We've contacted Caleb's parents, and he's at the hospital right now getting treatment," Tate explained.

He'd called Piper and Ethan over to the picnic table behind the cabin to discuss matters, while Stu administered new medication to Koko through an IV. As much as Piper worried about whether there was still enough time to save her wolf, she was more concerned about Caleb. Losing Koko would be a blow, one that would take a long, long time to accept. But being responsible for losing Caleb was something she couldn't even wrap her head around.

"Is he going to be okay?" she asked. *Please. Please, God. Let him be okay.*

Tate straightened a stack of manila folders he'd set on the table. The one on top was labeled "Aurora Wolf & Wildlife Sanctuary." She had a police file. Unreal. "Don't worry. He's going to be just fine. Since he only touched the flowers instead of ingesting them, the levels of toxins in his system are expected to be relatively small."

"Good." She nodded, dazed. Nothing felt real. None of it. She felt as if she was moving through a dream. A nightmare.

Ethan reached for her hand and gave it a squeeze. "Has Stu said anything about Koko's prognosis, Tate?"

His friend nodded and flipped open her file folder. "He seems to think the wolf stands a good chance, since he made it through the night and now we know what kind of poison we're dealing with."

Piper could have wept with relief, and very nearly did… until her gaze fell on a stack of photographs in the folder.

Tate kept talking while she stared at the images, utterly confused. At first she thought they must have ended up in her police file by accident. But then she realized the log cabin in the pictures was indeed hers, only it had been defaced in a way that made her blood run cold.

Killers.

Tate motioned to the contents of the folder. "The good news is that now we know the poisoning had nothing to do with the prior incident here at the sanctuary. It was just an accident."

"An accident," Piper echoed absently, unable to look away from the pictures.

There had to be some mistake. Those photos couldn't be real, could they? She would know if something so ugly, so vile had happened on her property.

"What are those?" she asked. Then louder, "Those photos. Where did they come from?"

Tate glanced at Ethan.

Ethan grew very still beside her.

Tate fixed his gaze on her once more. "Piper, these are the photographs from the graffiti incident last week."

"No." She shook her head. Maybe if she shook it hard enough, she could rattle those awful images right out of her mind.

"Piper." Ethan said her name with an exaggerated calmness that made her want to scream.

She remembered how touched she'd been that he'd painted the cabin for her. He'd found the paint and cleaned up the graffiti before she'd even seen it. And now she knew why.

She spun to face him. "You lied to me."

Tate rose from his seat. "Maybe I should give you two a minute. I'll go check on Stu and Koko."

"You lied to me, Ethan." She didn't care that Tate was still probably within earshot. She needed answers. Now.

Ethan sighed. "I'm sorry."

Those words that had meant so much only hours before now seemed wholly inadequate. How was that possible? "Someone painted the word *Killers* on my cabin, the place where I sleep every night, and you didn't think I had a right to know about it? You're *sorry?*"

"I should have told you. I *meant* to tell you." He swallowed. "Eventually."

She couldn't believe what she was hearing. No wonder he'd been in such a panic when she called 911 about Palmer. And no wonder she'd found him sleeping in his car. He'd been keeping watch over her. "You should have told me. Immediately. This wasn't your secret to keep, Ethan."

"Piper, you can trust me. I promise." The urgency in his voice was palpable. And real. So real that she wanted to believe it.

But she could already feel herself closing up, like a dying bloom. "Is there anything else you've been keeping from me?"

Tell me no. Please tell me no.

He took too long to answer. So long that she almost got up and left him sitting there by himself.

"Tell me, Ethan," she said, hating the way that her voice broke when she said his name.

He took a deep breath. "The inspector from the NNC came yesterday while you were with Koko. It looks like your grant may be getting denied."

She dropped her head to her hands. How much more bad news could she take in the course of twenty-four hours? Just when she thought things were getting better. Just when Koko had a glimmer of hope.

Just when she'd thought she'd fallen in love.

"Piper, you can appeal. I'll help you." Ethan placed a soothing hand on her back.

She shrugged it off. "I think you've done enough."

His gray eyes narrowed and grew gunmetal sharp. "What is that supposed to mean?"

"Look, I understand why you wrote the things you did in the paper. I still don't like it, but I understand now. Secrets and lies are another story." Her voice rose an octave. She could hear herself sounding slightly hysterical. Possibly even unreasonable, given the fact that Ethan had been the one who'd figured out how Koko had become poisoned.

He'd also been the one to stay with her all night. He'd been the one to make sure she was safe. Time and time again.

She swallowed. *The one.* Why did that phrase keep coming up? He couldn't be *the one.*

"I was trying to protect you. I didn't want to see you hurt," he murmured. "And did you really expect me to tell you about the NNC when you'd been sitting in the snow with a dying wolf in your lap all night long?"

She hated that his explanation sort of made sense. Truth was black-and-white. She shouldn't feel at all conflicted. Not after everything she'd been through.

"I need to know I can trust you," she whispered. "It's hard for me. You don't know how hard."

"You can trust me, lovely. I promise."

She wanted to. So badly. "Is there anything else? Anything else at all?"

"No." He shook his head. "There's not."

He opened his arms, and just as she was about to give in, just as she felt her resistance slipping away, Zoey came jogging up the trail from the direction of the reindeer farm.

"Here you are. I've been calling for the past half hour. You haven't been answering your phone." She bent over, out of breath. She must have run all the way from her place.

"Sorry, it's been a little crazy around here." Piper patted the empty spot next to her on the bench. "Sit down, and we'll fill you in."

"I can't. I'm late." She stood upright again and pointed at Ethan. "And so are you. That's why I've been calling all morning. Let's go, or we're going to miss our runway time. Thanks to Palmer, I'm not exactly the air traffic controller's favorite person. He wouldn't be happy if I threw a wrench in his entire schedule by being late."

What in the world was she talking about?

"Zoey, wait," Ethan started.

But he'd gone pale, and Piper knew she didn't want to hear whatever came next. In fact, she wanted to clamp her hands over her ears so she could keep believing she could trust him.

But she couldn't. She couldn't allow herself to be so foolish. Not again. "Will someone please tell me what's going on?"

Zoey frowned, clearly confused. "I'm scheduled to fly Ethan to Anchorage this morning to catch his commercial flight to Seattle."

Ethan dropped his head in his hands.

"Seattle? You're going to Seattle this morning?" Piper no longer felt hysterical. Or even angry.

Just disappointed. Maybe the most disappointed she'd ever been.

"I've got a job interview at *The Seattle Tribune* this afternoon, but I'd changed my mind." He leveled his gaze at her, and she had trouble focusing on anything other than the earnest gray of his eyes. "That's why I'm here. With you."

"Don't." She shook her head.

She couldn't take any more. No more secrets. No more explanations. No more feeling as if she loved this person who, as of yesterday, had been planning to leave.

She didn't know why she was surprised. Or even hurt. People always left. They always left and they always lied. She should have been used to it by now.

Zoey shifted her weight from one foot to the other. "Should I leave? I'm getting the feeling I should go."

"No," Piper said tersely. "Stay."

She stood up and willed her knees not to buckle. She needed to get away from here. Back to Koko. Back to where things made sense. "I thought you were different, Ethan. I really did."

"I am. I'm in love with you, Piper. I'm not him." Stephen's name rang in her ears, unspoken, but very much there.

I'm in love with you.

No one had ever said those words to her before. She'd longed to hear someone say they loved her for as long as she'd been alive. But she'd never expected it would come at a moment like this. A moment when she was hurt and confused and tired. So very tired.

I'm in love with you.

He sat there staring at her, waiting for her to respond.

I love you, too.

She wanted to say it. Ten minutes prior, she would have. But now she simply couldn't stomach it.

"Piper," Zoey whispered.

She should say something. Anything. She couldn't just keep standing there. Mute.

"I'm not him," Ethan repeated, his voice raspy around the edges. "I'm not that man."

She wrapped her arms around herself. Maybe she could hold herself together for a few more minutes. She could fall apart when he was gone. When it was just her and the wolves again. "No, you're not. You're the man who tried to get my wolf sanctuary closed down. You're the

man who wanted to run me and my wolves out of town."
He flinched, but she kept going, unable to stop the flow
of ugliness coming out of her mouth. "You, Ethan Hale,
are the man who tried to destroy my dream and then lied
to my face. So go. Go to Seattle. Go wherever you want,
but just go."

Then she spun around and turned her back on him so
she wouldn't have to see the wounds her words had in-
flicted.

Chapter Fifteen

"**W**ho's afraid of the big, bad wolf?" Piper whispered.

In the quiet shadows of the wings of the community center stage, Koko's ears twitched in response to her voice. Calm and content by her side, he was the antithesis of the big, bad wolf. Piper wished Ethan could see him now, the perfect gentleman actor, healed and whole, waiting for his big moment onstage.

Ethan wasn't standing beside her, of course. Piper didn't even know if he was anywhere in the building, seated among the audience or standing at the back of the crowded auditorium. She wholeheartedly doubted it.

She'd neither seen nor spoken to him since the morning after Koko had ingested the poison a full week ago. Ethan had respected her wishes and kept his distance from the sanctuary, taking her at her word when she'd said she'd no longer wanted anything to do with him. The morning after that first lonely day without him there, she'd driven into town for a copy of the *Yukon Reporter* out of pure, morbid curiosity. What had he written about Koko's illness? How had he spun things? Had he painted her as the crazy wolf woman who lived on a mountain and accidentally poisoned her pack? He could have printed a story like that. It would have been accurate. Sort of. She wouldn't have blamed him if he had. After the things she'd said to him, she deserved it. She deserved worse.

But that's not the kind of story he'd written. Instead he'd written nothing at all.

Not a word. Nothing about the wolfsbane. Nothing about Koko. Nothing about the vigil they'd kept under the pink Alaskan sky. In fact, she couldn't find a single article with his byline anywhere among the newspaper's many pages. She'd checked. Twice.

She couldn't believe it. It was over. At last. People were no longer debating the pros and cons of her wolf sanctuary over lattes at the coffee bar. She could flip through the local radio stations on her drive into town and not hear a single word about how she'd forced Ethan to clean out wolf pens. His front-page column had been replaced with coverage of the local mayoral debates. Business as usual. Piper and her wolves were no longer being mocked on a daily basis for the entire world to see. Or the state, at least. Tate had even located the kids who'd vandalized the cabin. They'd sent written apologies and were performing community service at the church.

Piper should have been thrilled.

"Is it crazy that I miss Ethan?" she said, not realizing she'd actually uttered the words aloud until Koko's ears pricked forward in attention. "Because I sort of do."

Now who's the liar?

She didn't just miss him a little bit. She missed him a lot. More than she'd ever missed anything or anyone in her entire life.

"Are you ready, Piper?" Zoey, whom Posy had appointed stage manager, poked her head through the curtain. "It's almost time."

"As ready as I'll ever be." Piper pasted on a smile, and

her gaze flitted to the small portion of the audience that was visible beyond the curtain. She couldn't make out anything from back here. She couldn't even tell how many rows of seats were occupied.

"And how's our superstar?" Zoey cooed at Koko.

Piper gave him a pat on his side, and noted that his weight seemed back to normal. She could no longer feel his ribs protruding through his thick coat. "As good as new and ready for his close-up."

"Great. Just stand by. I'll be directly opposite you in the wings, and I'll give you the thumbs-up signal once the girls have all moved offstage. Then you'll walk with Koko to center stage and take a bow. Easy peasy."

"Easy peasy," Piper repeated.

"Any questions?"

"Nope, it all seems really straightforward." She fiddled with Koko's leash, winding it around her hand, then unwinding it. "Except maybe just one thing."

"Yes?" Zoey asked. "What is it? Shoot."

"I was just wondering if, well…" Piper shook her head. This was silly. Of course he wasn't here. Zoey would have already told her if she'd seen him. Why would he come, anyway?

Piper had said such horrible things to him. Things she'd had no right to say.

You're the man who tried to get my wolf sanctuary closed down. You're the man who wanted to run me and my wolves out of town. You, Ethan, are the man who tried to destroy my dream and then lied to my face.

Of course he hadn't come to the dance recital. He'd probably never speak to her again, and she wouldn't blame him one bit.

Zoey shook her head. "He's not here, Piper. I'm sorry."

And there it was. Her answer. His absence spoke volumes, far more than his column had ever said. "I know. I was just hoping, I guess."

Maybe he'd moved on. Maybe he'd even gotten the job in Seattle. He'd missed the interview, but maybe somehow he'd had it rescheduled. She honestly had no idea what to think. One thing was sure—he wasn't writing anymore. At least not here in Alaska.

The music stopped, and the whisper of tiny slippered feet exiting the stage took its place.

"That's your cue!" Zoey's face lit up, thoughts of Ethan forgotten. For one of them, at least. "Get ready."

Piper took a deep breath, gathered Koko's leash in her hands and led him into the spotlight. Just the two of them. Just like always.

The roar of applause from the audience was so loud that it was a wall of noise. Koko blinked into the light with his cool copper eyes and leaned against her side. She was so proud of him then, so amazed at all that he'd overcome in order to be able to stand beside her and represent the strength and beauty of his resilient species.

She glanced down at him. Her boy.

He lowered his head, narrowed his eyes and fixed his gaze on something just behind her. Before she could stop him, he gathered his legs beneath him and sprang. The audience gasped as he landed on his intended prey with a thud and bit down hard.

There was a sound of paper tearing. Koko tossed his head, and green tissue paper leaves from the closest prop tree flew through the air like confetti.

"Really, Koko? Attacking the props?"

He pawed at the tree trunk he'd knocked over, and a few chuckles skittered through the seated crowd. Feeding off their energy, Koko's paws gained speed and soon he was shredding the tree. He looked like a dog—a very big, very goofy dog—trying to bury a bone.

"You are the world's biggest ham." Piper shook her head.

Laugher filled the auditorium as the curtain swished closed, and once again it was just the two of them. Center stage. It had all happened so fast.

Of course, that had been the plan all along, but it felt so strange now. Less than a minute onstage, when this appearance had caused such grief between her and Ethan.

She had to stop thinking about him. She couldn't go on like this. Missing him. Loving him.

Seeing him.

She blinked. Was she hallucinating, or was that really Ethan walking toward her from the wings?

"Nice job," he said, in that familiar voice that she still heard late at night when she closed her eyes and let herself remember. *I'm in love with you, Piper.*

It was him. In the flesh. "You came."

"I wouldn't have missed this, lovely." His lips curved into a smile that didn't quite reach his eyes. "I hope you don't mind."

She shook her head. "Of course I don't."

"Nice touch, terrifying everyone like that." He reached out and gave Koko a pat on the head.

Piper cleared her throat. "He was only playing."

"I was kidding, Piper. It was a joke." There was that sad smile again.

She swallowed. "I knew that."

"No, you didn't, but that's my fault." He nodded toward the green papier-mâché at Koko's feet. "Besides, I'm pretty sure that tree was made entirely out of my column. I think what we just witnessed was simply Koko's commentary on my work."

The hum of the audience had faded to silence. Lights flickered and dimmed. It was time to leave. Posy and Zoey would come looking for her any second.

Not yet. She wasn't ready. There was so much left to say. "I looked for your column in the paper and couldn't find it."

He shook his head. "I don't work for the *Yukon Reporter* anymore. I've been out of town."

"Oh, so you got the job in Seattle. Congratulations." She should be happy for him. She knew she should, but all she wanted to do was cry.

To her horror, she did.

A tear slid down her face, and Ethan brushed it away with the pad of his thumb. "No. I changed my mind about that, remember? I've been in Denali. I needed to go back there. I needed to make peace with what happened. It was time."

"And did you?"

"Yes, thanks to you." His gaze dropped to Koko standing calmly at her side. "You and your pack, that is."

"I've missed you, Ethan. I've missed you so much." She took a shuddering breath. She was crying in earnest now. She wouldn't have thought she'd have any tears left after the past week, but they were falling from her eyes faster than Ethan could wipe them away.

"Don't cry, lovely. I'm here." He pulled her close and whispered into her hair, "It's okay."

Koko whined. She tried to collect herself, but Ethan was here. And he was touching her and saying such nice things. Things she didn't deserve to hear. "But it's not, Ethan. I said such awful things to you. I'm sorry. I'm so sorry."

He held her even tighter against him. "We've both said things we wish we could retract."

She pulled back so she could look him in the eyes. "But you were there. You were always there, even when you wanted to leave. Even when I tried to push you away… you were there. No one's ever been there for me like that. No one."

He kissed her forehead and smiled. This time, it lit up his entire face. "Well, what kind of stalker would I be if I gave up so easily?"

His smile, his gentle laughter, was all the encouragement she needed to say the thing she most wanted to articulate. "Come back, Ethan. Come back to the sanctuary. Please. I need you there."

He shook his head. "No you don't. The tip jar out there is overflowing, thanks to Koko. I have a feeling you'll soon have more visitors at the sanctuary than you'll know what to do with. You and I both know you could handle things just fine without me." His voice was so tender that it almost made his refusal bearable.

"Oh." She nodded. Woodenly. "Okay."

He tipped her chin up so that her gaze was fixed with his, and in his eyes she saw the answer she'd been hoping for. *Yes.* "But I'd like to come back to the sanctuary anyway, if you'll have me."

"You would?"

"I would, but first I want you to take a look at something I've been working on the past few days." He reached into his jacket pocket, pulled out a thick envelope and offered it to her.

She handed him Koko's leash and opened the envelope. Inside she found a packet of papers with the NNC seal at the top. She recognized it at once, especially since she'd just received her rejection letter from their grant committee two days before. "What is this?"

"It's a revised NNC application for the sanctuary," he said quietly.

She flipped through the pages, which represented hours upon hours of work. How had he found time to put this together and also drive to Denali? He must have worked nonstop. "You did this? This is what you've been busy writing instead of your column?"

He nodded. "In order to reapply, the facility must show proof of a significant change in management. I want to be that change. I haven't filed the papers because this is your call. Your dream. No more secrets, Piper. You have my word on that. If the answer is no, I'll understand. I've been offered a job in Denali. At the park, like before. But I want to be here. I belong here. With you and the wolves."

Her tremulous orchid heart that had closed so quietly when she'd seen those photographs in the police file bloomed as if kissed by the sun itself. "You want to help me run the sanctuary? Full-time?"

It was more than she could have hoped for. More than she dreamed possible.

"I want to do more than that, lovely. I want to be part of your pack, if you'll have me. I love you, Piper. I always have, and I always will. I want to marry you. I want that more than I want my next breath."

This time, there was no stopping her response. The words rose from the very bottom of her soul, where they'd been waiting for the perfect time, the perfect man. That man was Ethan. "I love you, too. It would be an honor to marry you."

Koko pressed the weight of his wolfish frame against their legs. Ethan looked down at him and grinned. "I think I'm in."

"You are, my love. You are." All this time, Ethan had

been the missing piece. But he'd come back, and she was going to be his wife.

Her pack was complete.

At last.

Epilogue

YUKON REPORTER
News from the Last Frontier

Aurora Wolf and Wildlife Center Extends a Warm Welcome to New Resident from South of the Border
by reporter Ben Grayson

The Aurora Wolf and Wildlife Center welcomed a new member to its growing wolf pack yesterday. The sanctuary's most recent acquisition comes all the way from central Mexico and is a *Canis lupus baileyi*, more commonly known as a Mexican gray wolf. Mexican gray wolves are a critically endangered subspecies of the more common gray wolf, indigenous to the Southwest United States.

The new wolf, which the sanctuary staff has named Caleb in honor of its youngest employee, who was recently awarded a full scholarship to the University of Alaska, where he plans to study wildlife management, is expected to draw crowds from as far away as Denali and the remote northern city of Barrow. He is the sole Mexican gray wolf living in captivity in the state of Alaska, and one of only an estimated fifty of his species left in the world.

Said Aurora Wolf and Wildlife Center's founder and president, Piper Quinn, "It is an honor to provide sanctuary to a magnificent and treasured animal such as our newest boy, Caleb. Our ability to care for critically endangered species like the Mexican gray wolf is due to our recent accreditation from the National Nature Conservatory. I'm happy to announce that we've also been approved as one of only five facilities in the country to initiate a breeding program designed to save endangered species. So Caleb will be getting a girlfriend in the near future, and if all goes well, our wildlife center should see our first litter of pups by the end of the year."

Perfect timing. Piper and her husband, Ethan Hale, the sanctuary's operations manager, are expecting their first child on Christmas Day. Our sources say it's a girl!

* * * * *

Dear Reader,

Welcome back to the wintry, romantic world of Aurora, Alaska!

As you'll see, Aurora is now home to a wolf sanctuary, which I know is a bit of an unusual setting. Last summer, I visited a wolf and wildlife refuge in Divide, Colorado. It was a wonderful experience. The refuge was nestled in a lovely, serene forest, and getting to experience hands-on interaction with the rescued wolves is something I'll never forget. I left the wolf sanctuary that day knowing I simply had to write about it. So that's the story of how this book came about.

I love writing about animals. You may have noticed there are pets of some kind in every book I write. I have three dogs of my own, and every one of them is spoiled rotten. (In the sweetest of ways. I promise!) As much as I love animals, they can't take the place of the love and affection of another human being. People need each other. That need is what *Alaskan Sanctuary* is about at its core. It's about love and family. It's about trust and healing.

And yes, it's about wolves, too.

If this is the first of my Alaskan books that you've read, I hope you enjoy yourself, and I hope you'll also consider reading the other books in this series—*Alaskan Hearts*, *Alaskan Hero*, *Sleigh Bell Sweethearts* and *Alaskan Homecoming*.

Thank you so much for reading! I appreciate all of my readers so much. Each and every one of you. See you back in Alaska soon.

Best wishes,
Teri Wilson

REQUEST YOUR FREE BOOKS!

2 FREE INSPIRATIONAL NOVELS
PLUS 2
FREE
MYSTERY GIFTS

Love Inspired®

LI15

"That's James," Sara the matchmaker explained in English. "He's the one charging me an outrageous amount for the addition to my house."

"You want craftsmanship, you have to pay for it," James answered confidently. He strode into the kitchen, opened a cupboard, removed a coffee mug and poured himself a cup. "We're the best, and you wouldn't be satisfied with anyone else."

He glanced at Mari. "This must be your new houseguest. Mari, is it?"

"*Ya*, this is my friend Mari." Sara introduced her. "She and her son, Zachary, will be here with me for a while, so I expect you to make her feel welcome."

"Pleased to meet you, Mari," James said. The foreman's voice was pleasant, his penetrating eyes strikingly memorable. Mari felt a strange ripple of exhilaration as James's strong face softened into a genuine smile, and he held her gaze for just a fraction of a second longer than was appropriate.

Warmth suffused her throat as Mari offered a stiff nod and a hasty "Good morning," before turning her attention to her unfinished breakfast. Mari didn't want anyone to get the idea that she'd come to Seven Poplars so Sara could find her a husband. That was the last thing on her mind.

"Going to be working for Gideon and Addy, I hear," James remarked as he added milk to his coffee from a small pitcher on the table.

Mari slowly lifted her gaze. James had nice hands. She raised her eyes higher to find that he was still watching her intently, but it wasn't a predatory gaze. James seemed genuinely friendly rather than coming on to her, as if he was interested in what she had to say. "I hope so." She suddenly felt shy, and she had no idea why. "I don't know a thing about butcher shops."

"You'll pick it up quick." James took a sip of his coffee. "And Gideon is a great guy. He'll make it fun. Don't you think so, Sara?"

Sara looked from James to Mari and then back at James. "I agree." She smiled and took a sip of her coffee. "I think Mari's a fine candidate for all sorts of things."

Don't miss
A HUSBAND FOR MARI
by Emma Miller,
available February 2016 wherever
Love Inspired® books and ebooks are sold.

SPECIAL EXCERPT FROM

Love Inspired HISTORICAL

Can a grieving woman find happiness with a man who can't remember his own name?

Read on for a sneak preview of
RECLAIMING HIS PAST,
an exciting new entry in the series,
SMOKEY MOUNTAIN MATCHES.

October 1885
Gatlinburg, Tennessee

It wasn't easy staying angry at a dead man.

Jessica O'Malley hesitated in the barn's entrance, the tang of fresh hay ripening the air. The horses whickered greetings from their stalls, beckoning her inside, probably hoping for a treat. She used to bring them carrots and apples. She used to enjoy spending time out here.

This place had become the source of her nightmares. Her gaze homed in on the spot where the man she'd loved had died defending her. The bloodstain was long gone, but the image of Lee as she'd held him during those final, soul-wrenching moments would be with her for as long as she lived.

If he'd been honest with her, if he'd made different choices, she wouldn't be living this lonely, going-through-the-motions half-life. She wouldn't be a shadow of her former self, clueless how to reclaim the fun-loving girl she once was.

Lost in troubling memories, a weak cry for help wrenched her back to the present with a thud. Her empty milk pail slipping from her fingers, Jessica hurried to investigate. She surged around the barn's exterior corner and had to grope the weathered wall for support at the unexpected sight of a bruised and battered man near the smokehouse.

Hatless and looking as if he'd romped in a leaf pile, his golden-blond hair was messy. "Can you help me?"

"Who are you? What do you want?"

He dropped to his knees, one hand outstretched and the other clutching his side. Jessica belatedly noticed the blood soaking through his tattered shirt. Bile rose into her throat. Lee's gunshot wound had done the same to his clothing. There'd been so much. It had covered her hands. Her dress. Even the straw covering the barn floor had been drenched with it.

"Please…ma'am…"

The distress in his scraped-raw voice galvanized her into action. Searching the autumn-draped woods fanning out behind her farm's outbuildings, she hurried to his side and ducked beneath his arm. She barely had time to absorb the impact of his celestial blue eyes on hers. "What happened to you?"

"I…don't remember."

Don't miss
RECLAIMING HIS PAST
by Karen Kirst,
available February 2016 wherever
Love Inspired® Historical books and ebooks are sold.